GeeCee

AI WAITS FOR NO ONE

a novel by

EDWARD M. KRAUSS

EABooks Publishing
Your Partner In Publishing

GEECEE, AI Waits for No One
Copyright @ 2025 Edward M Krauss

The language used in this book is at the author's request and does not reflect the publishing policies of EA Books Publishing.

ISBN: 978-1-966382-12-6
LCCN: 2025904581

Cover design: Rachel Ford-Cooper
Cover photo: ©Azza-Studios via Canva.com

Published by EABooks Publishing, a division of
Living Parables of Central Florida, Inc. a 501c3
EABooksPublishing.com

For the loved ones of my small but splendid family,
for the loved ones in Esther's larger and also splendid family,
and of course for Esther, for innumerable reasons.

The cast of characters in this novel appears at the end

Not many years from now . . .

CHAPTER ONE

The truck sat in a small warehouse that had been quietly converted into a laboratory on the west side of Bakersfield, California. The vehicle was nondescript; the usual DOT markings on the door, Walt's Forward Trucking on the tractor and trailer sides. A bit of dried mud here and there, some scratches. A standard, normal diesel tractor, except the windows had a slight, almost undetectable dark tint making it a bit harder to see the driver's hands and arms. The other modifications were the cameras and GPS.

On top of the cab, and at the front above the bumper, and on the sides of the cab were small boxes, only four inches high. A similar box sat at the rear center top of the trailer. The side, back and rear boxes overhung the trailer by a few inches.

Walter 'Walt' Wizniski, chief project engineer, walked toward the truck, opened the door and looked in, glancing at the computer. Ellen Michel followed him. Walt held the door for her as she climbed in. She buckled her seat belt, leaned back, looked at Walt and said, "Ready." He nodded, closed the door and stepped back a few feet. She turned the key that was already in the ignition and the four hundred fifty-five horsepower diesel engine started up. It was a low mileage, fully tuned engine and idled quietly.

It was a typical truck interior, with a few modifications. On the passenger-side floor was a small computer connected to the truck's power source, and a camera aimed upward at the driver's position. On the top of the steering column was a small microphone, only slightly larger than the average lavaliere mic, on a swivel mount that allowed it to be tilted upward toward the driver's face. There was a large toggle switch, no label, that would flip up or down. It was in the up position. Below that was a toggle switch that went left-right. Left was labeled *Broadcast On* and right for *Broadcast Off*; the switch was to the left. A seven-inch square screen was positioned to the driver's right, below window height but high enough that it took only a quick glance to see it.

It was a Sunday evening, just after sundown, the day and time with low truck traffic; the planned round trip just over a hundred miles. The warehouse door slid upward, and Ellen instinctively reached toward the wheel with her left hand, her right hand toward the shift lever, then she drew her hands back and laid them in her lap.

The truck began to move. The driver felt a touch of panic and took two deep breaths; she knew what was happening, had spent hours discussing it, but still the actual event was scary, exhilarating. The truck drove slowly through the paved lot, then a gate, turned right and went two hundred yards to a stop sign. Ellen's foot hovered over the brake, her hand near the large toggle switch, ready to flip it down and take control of the vehicle, but the truck began to slow properly before coming to the intersection, applying the brakes smoothly. She glanced at the screen showing what was behind her from the camera mounted high on the rear of the trailer; with a touch of a button she could see the camera views to left and right. After waiting for cross traffic the truck started up again. She couldn't help it, quickly glanced left and right, but knew as she did so there wouldn't be any approaching vehicles. Another quarter mile and the truck entered the ramp to take I-5 north. Ellen relaxed more, noticing how smoothly the truck worked up through the gears until reaching fifty-five, the speed limit for trucks, not often obeyed. Nothing happened for the first half-hour; the truck sat at exactly fifty-five in the right lane, usually being passed. Some music would have been welcome now, but the radio was only a two-way communication system connected to the engineers and software designers, using the *Broadcast* setting. The instructions were to have no messages unless there was a problem; none had occurred so no speaking from either Ellen or the research team who could, of course, see everything she could—actually more, a wide telemetry range.

Up ahead, Ellen could see the red rollers of a California Highway Patrol car on the right shoulder. She glanced in her left side mirror to see if she could pull over one lane, but as she did so Ellen felt the truck slow, downshifting, until the car in the left lane passed, then the truck turned on its left-turn signal, slid over one lane and stayed there until it had passed the patrol car and the officer talking to the driver of a low-slung two-seater. "Way over eighty, likely" Ellen thought, not really noticing how the truck signaled to return to the right lane, once more at fifty-five.

That was it, an uneventful trip; the truck leaving the highway, crossing over at an overpass then heading back in the return direction. Once it left the highway the truck went through a green light, stopped at a red light, turned at two intersections and finally pulled into the waiting, open doors of the destination. She climbed down from the cab as the engineers approached her from the office where they had monitored the trip. Serious men and women—there were no shouts or loud laughter, just handshakes, smiles, nodding heads. Partly this was because they weren't surprised; everything had gone as they expected from their repeated tests . . . and partly because they knew this could be the start of the elimination of hundreds of thousands of jobs. Perhaps a million or more, a million or more Americans suddenly out of work.

CHAPTER TWO

Six weeks earlier

Tennic Personnel Services was located on the fifteenth floor of a starkly modern office building in downtown Bakersfield. It was a highly rated recruitment company, in business over twenty years. Frank Stevenson sat down with the president of Tennic Personnel Services, Susan Tennic. She was, he guessed, in her mid-fifties, and carried herself with friendly competence. Frank immediately felt he had selected the right firm for this task. "Ms. Tennic . . . "

"Please call me Susan. How can I help you?"

"Susan, Frank. What I'd like your company to do is conduct an unusual personnel search in absolute confidence."

"Certainly, that's how we always operate. How high a level are you looking for, what position and salary range?"

"A long haul truck driver."

Susan tilted her head, a puzzled look on her face. "A truck driver? We only do professional searches. I'm sorry, I don't understand."

"I came to you because your company has a good reputation, we checked. The situation is we need a very special person for a highly unusual situation, assignment. All I can tell you is that it is absolutely legal. Nothing more."

"Go on."

"We need someone with the requisite CDL, that is, a commercial driver's license. The driver has to be in good standing, a clean driving record or, at worst, a minor offense, maybe two, but not recent. In other words, a good, experienced driver that any trucking company would be glad to hire. I know that this isn't your usual search . . . "

"That's for sure . . . "

"But we can't run a want ad. It is a driving assignment that we want to keep under wraps as long as possible. And another thing— it would also be helpful if the person were somewhat hurting financially. That is, we're not looking to steal a highly successful, well-paid driver from a company, but rather someone with limited ties and a real need to make a buck. An honest buck, I assure you, but a situation a top driver with a good income might well turn down."

"Man oh man, I am seriously intrigued. Frank, I don't turn down business. I'll take the assignment, but we'll have to discuss our fee. We charge twenty-three percent of the find's . . . that's what we call the accepted recruit, the find . . . twenty-three percent of the find's first year salary. So unless you're planning on paying top management wages to your driver we'd have to reach some other agreement."

"So forty thousand up, maybe sixty or more, that's your fee, right?"

"On occasion over one hundred, but usually in that range, yes."

"How about fifty thousand, flat fee?"

"Done. I'm taking this on partly for the fee, thank you, but also because it will take me, our team, into some recruiting a long way from our usual beat."

Frank nodded. "I can appreciate that. I'm guessing you'll get lots of questions from your staff. All you can tell them is what you're looking for, not the company name, not my name. And forgive me; I assume your staff keeps things confidential . . . . "

"Absolutely."

"But this is so . . . quirky? . . . that someone might be tempted to talk about it at a bar or party. Can't happen."

Susan opened her hands, a smile on her face. "Sounds like 'Loose Lips Sink Ships' from World War Two. Seriously, I'll stress it. How soon do you need your driver?"

"As soon as possible."

Susan sighed, reached across the desk to shake hands. "The old 'Yesterday is soon enough.' We're used to it, everyone in this industry is."

Two weeks later Susan called. "Frank, I believe we've found someone. Two surprises. The first is that I believe we have found just the right candidate in this short time. I think that's because the people I assigned were really into it; a totally different task than the usual suit search, plus some luck. Second, she's a woman."

"Well done. How soon can we interview her? And what's her name?"

"Ellen Michel, like the old Beatles song. M I C H E L. You don't seem very surprised that our candidate is a female. I thought almost all drivers of big trucks were men."

"Still the vast majority, but like personnel, law, medicine, the number, the percent, of women is increasing. The modern rigs are so much easier to drive with power steering, cruise control, automatic transmissions. Of course it is still a demanding occupation, I'm not minimizing it, but a woman who is a good car driver can certainly become a good truck driver. The percent of women is now somewhere around ten or fifteen percent, going up."

"Interesting. Really didn't know that. So . . . when and where for the interview?"

"Your place, if I may."

They agreed, Susan scheduled the meeting.

Four days later, approaching the office building housing Tennic Personnel Services, Frank Stevenson felt like a character in a spy novel; he hoped no one he knew saw him coming into the building, worse, going into Tennic's offices. He wanted no questions, no leaks. He was pleased that the recruiters had come through so quickly, although he knew it could be a good but failed try. He liked Susan and her upbeat but calm attitude. He also liked the firm's taste in modern art. There were no cute posters, no "The only thing missing from s-ccess is you!"—just comfortable furniture and a quiet, professional atmosphere.

Susan Tennic met Frank at the elevator, said hello but no more, and guided him to a small windowless conference room, complete with comfortable chairs, a polished wooden table, water and coffee. Waiting there was a woman. Susan introduced them.

"Frank, please meet Ellen Michel. She hasn't been given your last name, and understands this is a highly confidential meeting."

"Thank you." Susan then left them, closing the door quietly but firmly.

"Ellen, I'll get right to the reason for this interview. I'm going to ask you some hard questions about a possible driving assignment, a highly confidential one but an assignment I assure you is absolutely legal. If we select you you'll know my last name, the name of my company, where I work. So no secrets if you're our choice. OK?"

Ellen nodded, said nothing.

"If you were in a situation where you could make two hundred thousand in a few months, likely six at the most, but your efforts could result in hundreds of thousands of truck drivers being laid off, jobs gone, would you take the job? Would you do it?"

She stared hard at him. He waited.

"I'd sure have to think about it. My ex left me with credit card debt, upside-down mortgage. Only good thing about him is he's gone. Kids grown and gone too, on their own, that's good, don't have to see their mama driving her ass off. Oh, we keep in touch, but they got no real idea how I'm living. Sold the house, finally paid off what was left of the mortgage, sure glad about that, credit cards almost done and pitched except keep one, but not a lot for a retirement, not enough to quit when I'd like to. Living cheap, saving every damn penny I can. Two hundred for six months work? Gotta be illegal, I'm thinking. Can't do that, can't lose my license, driving's only way I know make good money."

"No, as I said, it is perfectly legal, and if we hire you you'll know every-thing. But I repeat, you have to hear this and get it, this work could mean *hundreds of thousands, or more,* of truckers never get behind the wheel again. And likely you'd be known, almost a sure thing. Could be national publicity. You could have people hating you, I want you to know that. You could be in danger. People out of work, they'd blame you, it could get really ugly."

"Won't they blame you too?"

"Good point. Yes, blame and danger enough for all of us. But you'd be the prime target. I have to tell you that."

"Why?"

"Remember you've signed a confidentiality agreement. Sorry, but I have to say that. If you decide not to do this that's your choice, but whether it is yes or no you can't say anything to anyone. Well, once it is announced publicly you can, but not before or we'll send a posse of lawyers to get you."

"Understood. I signed it. I mean it when I sign something."

"Good. Thanks. Well, here it is. We are developing a self-driving eighteen-wheeler. No human, just electronics, GPS, cameras. Amazing software to run it all. If it works, and we're pretty sure it will, a lot of jobs will disappear."

"Wow. Wow." She looked down, shook her head.

"So you're saying no?"

"No, no, just amazed, just trying to get to it. This is like those cars they've been working on for a while, ain't it, self-driving things?"

"Yes, same idea, just more stuff, enough to handle a long haul truck going thousands of miles, all kinds of roads, all kinds of conditions. Right now we are certain it can do just fine in clear weather, daytime, still working on nights and rain and fog and snow, but we're close to resolving all those, too, have the technology right in a month or less. We believe the final version will be able to well handle anything a human driver could."

"So I do what? What do you need me for?"

"You'll sit in the truck. We have to have a driver with a CDL, especially when we go to the feds, the government folks for a test. No way in hell they'll let us take it on the road without a driver. So you'll sit there, we'll have cameras on you all the time to prove you aren't steering or shifting or anything, just sitting there. You'll have a switch you can throw to take back control of the truck, turn off the system and give everything back to you, but we're guessing . . . no, we're about as sure as we can be that you'll never have to touch that switch. So you'll sit there, the cameras will record that the truck is driving, not you. That's it."

"I get it now. The target thing. I'll be the driver who sold out all the other drivers. I'll be the trash that put thousands of drivers out of work. I'll be hated, you bet."

"Yes. But not thousands. Hundreds of thousands. If this really works, if it works in all conditions, all weather, maybe over a million."

"A million drivers. Fuck! Sorry, excuse me."

"I've heard it before. And I agree. This is big, maybe the biggest thing since the Model T. Difference being that created jobs, this will eliminate jobs." He paused, got up, paced a bit. Ellen waited. "The thing is, it eliminates the driver jobs. There will be jobs for electricians and software people and hardware installers and computer geeks up the wazoo. Problem is they all need advanced educations, all those jobs call for some training—or a lot. Same thing happened when they started installing those scanners in grocery stores. Fewer jobs for checkout folks, but more jobs for, well, same list, computer people and installers and all that. Or banks. Automatic tellers, not so many teller jobs, but how about those machines that can pay you, count it out in a flash. I've never gotten an extra twenty, never heard of anyone who has. Maybe somewhere a time or two, but think about the engineering to design and build a money counter, money dispenser, then someone to maintain it. Skills. So there will be new jobs, but not jobs a trucker with no other skills can move into."

While he was talking she had been listening, but also thinking, weighing. "Three hundred, and I'm your girl. I'm thinking I might have to move away, could be a lot of people want to fry my ass. Maybe out of the country for a while, wouldn't mind that, never been to England or France or any of those places. Hell, I might learn French and live there, who knows. My name, Michel, comes from French people, way back, buncha generations ago. Started using it back up when me and my old man busted. Yah, could be France. Three and it's a deal."

He nodded. "I think I can make that happen. I'll get back to you in two days, maybe sooner."

"That's fine, I'm on the road six tomorrow morning, be gone for four days. Always got my cell phone with me though, in a holder, can chat with you with both hands on the wheel. So maybe, if you say yes to the three, we meet in about a week?"

"Sure. And to avoid suspicion, you'd have to give your employer two weeks notice, right?"

"No, I'm independent, we drivers come and go all the time, sorta like part-time taxi drivers . . . we say we're available, the company says when they'll need us. I volunteer about as much as any, push the reg limits to the max.

"Which are? I really don't know . . . "

"Kinda complicated, but the one I stick with is eleven hours on the road, gotta rest ten. Then eleven again. So gas up, get food in the cab, cold drinks in a cooler, push that baby down the road for eleven."

"Eleven sounds like a bear to me . . . "

"You get used to it. Music, listen to the radio, pick up NPR almost anywhere. Sometimes rock, but that wears thin after some hours. Gotta stop and pee, gas up maybe, not often . . . hell, drive New York to San Fran, gas up, diesel that is, once on the trip, still got plenty when you arrive."

"I'm guessing you make it sound easier than it really is. No way in hell I could drive eleven hours. Maybe when I was a teenager. . . . "

"I want some good life when this is over, so I give myself rules. One is I almost never eat at the truck stops; if I do it is some soup or salad, no bacon or burgers or mayo. Bring my own healthy food. Also I work out every morning. Got some weights and those stretch bands at home, stretch bands in my travel bag, get up early enough every morning, *every morning*, put in twenty to thirty minutes. Have to eat right and exercise or a trucker risks dying early. Hell, I'm past early, so I have to take care of this body. Wanna hear something else? Kinda gross…."

"Sure."

"Another one of those times when it is easier to be a man than a woman. I mean, you're in the woods, hiking, no one else around, gotta pee. What do you do? Never mind, I know. Harder problem for us girls. Well, same thing on a long haul. For girls it is just too hard to pee while hauling ass at sixty or so. But you guys, hell, whip it out, use a milk jug, keep on truckin'. If the guy's a real asshole he flings it out of truck when thinks no one is looking, or just what the hell takes a chance on getting busted. Truck bombs, they call them. Sick. Some dudes are just sick assholes. Sorry, getting carried away . . . "

"Not at all, you just added to my knowledge base. Could have done without that knowledge" he said, laughing "but thanks."

Like almost all drivers, Ellen was usually pushing five hundred miles a day. Her tractor lease, plus insurance, came to just over two thousand a month, but her income far exceeded that, and she was paying off the last of her debts while saving as much as she could each month.

The next morning Ellen woke at three, did her exercise routine, showered, ate two cold hardboiled eggs, applesauce, coffee, water, toast, and her usual one thousand milligrams of vitamin C and a vitamin B complex. As she told Frank, she was determined to someday, someday, have a healthy and happy retirement. She ate well and kept a pillow and blanket in her sleeper cab, found she could easily sleep, not disturbed by the sounds of rumbling trucks coming and going throughout the night.

At four-thirty Ellen did her usual walk-around of the leased truck. She checked the oil, best done when the engine has been off for hours and is cold, gave a small tug to the cable support springs and made certain the cables were securely plugged into her cab and the trailer. She loaded her cooler, filled with apples, oranges already quartered, celery, bottles of water. In her duffel bag were light and heavy gloves, aspirin, toilet paper, soap, shampoo, deodorant, toothbrush, toothpaste, mouthwash, exercise stretch bands, plus two clothing changes. After completing a few more inspections she got behind the wheel and started the engine, scanned all the gauges which were black and white in the daylight but glowed blue at night, put the automatic transmission into gear and the truck started to roll.

Two days later Frank called Ellen.

"Where are you?"

"Picked up a load at the Los Angeles docks, heading north, drops in Red Bluff and Redding, pick up a load there to bring back to Bakersfield. California down then up then down."

"Still interested in the job?"

"Three big ones, yes?"

"Yes. I can give you some investment advice, if you want it. But the short is you'll never have to work another day."

"It occurred to me that if this thing really works there will be unemployed French truckers, too. May have to change my name again. But worth it, worth it."

"Next Thursday morning a dark blue Subaru Legacy will pull up in front of your home at exactly nine. The driver's name is Walt. He is an engineering whiz—we couldn't do this without him. Feel free to ask him anything about the technology. You live alone, right?"

"Yep, plan to stay that way for a while. You men are trouble. Well, not you. . . ."

"Yes we can be. The reason I'm asking is whether anyone will ask who that man picking you up is, where you're going."

"Low-rent, one bedroom in a cheapo apartment complex. Paying off debts, saving, remember? Nobody to give a half a shit where I go. Sorry, gotta stop that talk if I'm going to be around your folks."

"Hold back on it now if you want to, soon you'll be able to say whatever you want to wherever you decide to go. Oh, and pack enough for an overnight, you'll be staying at a motel close to our operation. Nothing fancy, but safe. You'll be on the road the next day, test drive."

Walt picked up Ellen as planned, exactly at nine. He said "Hello, Ellen" and she answered "Hello, Walt" but there was nothing further for almost five minutes. Then she turned to him and asked "If something goes wrong how do I take control of the truck? And how quickly?"

"The truck—her name is GeeCee, I'll explain in a moment—GeeCee has a toggle switch on the dash in easy reach. You right-handed?"

"Yes."

"The switch is near the wheel, near your right hand. You can hit it without leaning forward, that's the way we mounted it. Of course if it isn't in a comfortable location for you just say so, we'll move it. The point is we want you to know that from your seat you can just flick a toggle and the system is off, off before you lift your finger from the switch. It goes from all GeeCee to all Ellen in an instant."

"There are cameras, right? That's how the tru . . . GeeCee sees."

"Yes, scanning in all directions, and GPS, and some other gadgets still being tweaked. But cameras are a big part of it, read speed limit signs, red or green lights, railroad crossing . . . every sign you can think of, actually"

"What about signs that are dirty or bent? What about detours?"

"There is constant feedback to a central location. We don't know yet how many trucks one person can monitor, but it is certainly a dozen or more, because most trips will go smoothly. If the truck isn't sure what to do it alerts the monitoring person—right now we're calling then wranglers, probably stick with that name—and that person can respond, even steer, drive the truck if need be. But to answer your question, the technology is similar to that used by the post office for thirty years or more . . . . it reads and translates signs, just as the post office computers can read close to 100% of the envelopes, even chicken-scratch writing, the truck's computers can read signs with letters missing or bent or . . . ."

"So if there is a detour?"

A shrug. "The truck will follow the detour signs. It's only one word, when the computer sees that word it obeys. But even more . . . . let's say a sign for some reason is wrong or missing. Situation where there should have been a turn in the middle of some small town, following a state route, but the sign is gone and the truck keeps going straight. Two things will happen then—the computer will notice that it hasn't seen any state route signs for a mile or so, we're still tweaking that distance, and at the same time the GPS will be sending alerts if the road is going away from the destination."

"So that's a situation where the wrangler might be needed, right? Country road, not sure where to turn or how to get back to the correct route. And ain't wrangler a cowboy word?"

"Yes, wranglers manage horses, take care of them, but seems to fit. Horsepower, you know. Corny. For your question, you use GPS when you're driving?"

"Not much, I know the docks and rail yards and companies pretty well, but sure, I use it. Neat."

"So don't forget how sophisticated GPS is. Online maps and all that. The truck will know it is going the wrong way, will look for roads back to where it wants to go, will just make the turns and get there, same as a human would who got lost. Use the electronic devices, say 'I'm here, how do I get from here to there?' and act on the information. If there is a load limit for trucks it can read and obey that sign. In a jam, confusion, the computer will notify the wrangler, but we figure about one hundred percent of the time in a situation like that the handler will just watch. Oh, and this is cool. The information about the correct turn will be stored in the database, so whether or not the sign is replaced the next truck will turn at that corner, the correct corner, sign or not."

"That is indeed cool. Lots."

"So about the name. We had this meeting, full team meeting, I'm saying we have got to have a name for the truck. Can't keep calling it that, the truck. If I had a good name I'd have given it a push, but didn't, just knew she was a lady. Like a ship, you know? I asked for suggestions, got Gertie, Robot, Doom, Lady T, bunch of junk. So then I say something like 'Funny, just wonderful. Come on folks, this truck is a game changer for the whole industry.' And that's when it happened. One of our engineers says 'How about Game Changer?' Not a lady name,

I'm thinking, but then another one, one of our female engineers, says 'How about G C?' So I ask how she spells it, and first she says g period c period. Then she says 'Wait, how about g e e c e e, one word but caps the g and c. GeeCee.' And that's it, that's the story."

CHAPTER THREE

After GeeCee's initial trip, only one hundred miles, the engineers and software experts had gone over the results, and the truck's electronic equipment, to the smallest detail. They had monitored the entire trip through telemetry and camera images, but went over it again, adding a few tweaks to the software. They sent it out for a few more trips, increasing the distance each time to two hundred miles or so, and then decided it was ready for a daytime trip in heavier traffic. A busy traffic day, many trucks on the road, again with Ellen Michel behind the wheel, not touching it. As soon as she arrived she told those waiting crew "I was photographed, heading south on I-5. Some guy up on an overpass. Looked like a big camera, you know, professional."

At a meeting the next morning, Frank Stevenson, CEO of the investment firm MHR Investors, LLC said "It's disappointing news, not because someone spotted the truck but because it happened so damn soon. We all expected that a truck with unusual fittings front, back and sides would attract attention, but would have liked it a little further in the process. Oh well, that's the deal now. The good news is that things are going great, just great. Thank you all. So we're going to move up the time table, get through our test steps quicker than we planned, do nighttime runs real soon. But two important reminders: Don't let quality or attention to little details slip because of this speedup. If you see a problem, say so! Don't ever think you're hurting the team by holding up a stop sign. You're hurting the team if you don't insist on perfection or as close as humanly possible. There are millions riding on this . . . many millions. We screw up and it will be years before this can be launched again. Second reminder, remember you all signed confidentiality pledges, and if you break them the investors will ... will ... life won't be pleasant. Sorry, got to say that. Oh, guess there is another reminder. Ten thousand dollar bonus to everyone on the payroll the day we get federal approval to run our equipment on the highway."

The picture taker Ellen had spotted was James R. Dorfmann, a professional photographer and occasional stringer for the *Bakersfield True Post*. He had a difficult decision to make: If he sent the photo and a story to the Post they likely would run it, but then it would be national news, no reason for anyone in Washington, in the highway administration, to pay any attention to him. Or he could meet with the Washington people first, tell them about what he saw, what he believed was happening, but by doing so taking the chance on being scooped by another reporter-photographer. He decided he wanted the power connection more, and so requested a meeting on the other side of the country as soon as possible.

Stewart W. Timmerlee grew up in Sacramento California, got involved in local politics where he earned a reputation as a decent, honest politician. That in turn led to election as a representative in Washington, where he served quietly but well. After two terms as a representative he made a run at senator. He lost in a close election, but as a reward for his loyal service the President appointed him Administrator of the National Highway Traffic Safety Administration.

One day in late October his secretary, the highly efficient Frieda Shippens, told him that there was a man coming from Bakersfield who wanted to meet with him, that it concerned interstate highway truck traffic. Frieda did the usual background check. His name was James R. Dorfmann, he was a resident of the city, self-employed as a photographer, primarily weddings and other happy events, on occasion freelance pictures picked up by the *Bakersfield True Post*. He also sold pictures to smaller newspapers and occasionally wrote columns for them and for the Post. No police record except for some traffic stops, usually for speeding. And no clue why he was interested in interstate highways.

Stewart Timmerlee's experience with unknown people who say they must meet with him on an urgent matter, who won't agree to meet with his staff, is to make them wait two weeks and then give them fifteen minutes at 8:30 in the morning, usually a Monday morning. Since he was almost always in his office by 8:00 he could afford the time, and on occasion the bad news carriers failed to show. If this guy really wanted to see him he'd be there on time, 5:30 California time. But this one showed up, actually standing outside the office door with his VISITOR badge around his neck when Frieda arrived; she asked him to take a seat and wait. Frieda went into Stewart's office, where he was looking at the daily schedule she had printed out and put on his desk at the end of the previous work day. He would fold it and keep it in his suit coat until he went home that evening.

He looked up. "Remind me, who is James R. Dorfmann?"

"He said he has information about a highway situation, interstate trucking, came all the way from California, wants to talk only to you, not staff. I gave him fifteen minutes."

Stewart nodded. "OK, let me know if he shows."

"He's here. Eager."

"Let's do it. Fifteen, right?"

She nodded and turned toward the door. She opened it and said "Mr. Dorfmann, please come in." As he entered she said "Administrator Timmerlee, Mr. Dorfmann."

Stewart stood up and shook hands, two firm grips meeting over his desk. "Please be seated, Mr. Dorfmann. How can I help you?"

The visitor paused a moment then opened a nine by twelve envelope and took out several pictures which he silently handed over. They showed an eighteen-wheeler, a typical long-haul truck, shot from above. Some were of the whole truck, some of the trailer, or just the back of the trailer. One showed the cab and driver. The Administrator looked at each in turn, then looked across the desk.

"I'm guessing you know who I am, what I do."

"Yes, we did a background check."

The visitor nodded. "So I work for myself, lots of different assign-ments, some free-lance for the newspapers, and I do some writing for them. I'm always on the lookout for an unusual picture, cute or scary or whatever. Listen to police calls in my car, get pics of fire fighters, police, people screaming or crying . . . papers buy that stuff. Occasional cute kid or dog or something like that. Anyway, I'm always looking, keeping an eye out. Write some articles now and then."

Stewart nodded.

"So one day, just dumb luck, I'm out real late. Did a wedding and reception, then get in my car and I'm almost home when I hear about a warehouse fire, so I turn around and head for it. Crazy business, this free-lancing. It was a waste, just smoke and a few firemen—sorry, learn-ing to say firefighters—hosing down a building. No excitement. Flames make a good night picture, but none."

Stewart shifted in his chair, a signal of impatience, but said nothing.

"Anyway, dumb luck, here comes this truck toward me. This is kinda rare, don't usually see trucks late on a Sunday night. Anyway, I'm at a stop sign, this truck comes into the intersection on the cross street. There's two streetlights on that corner, so I'm looking at it, wait-ing, and I notice this box, small box on the top of the cab, then another on the side, and another at the back of the trailer, but I'm not sure I saw everything. No idea what those boxes are. It's moving slow, 25 mile zone, looks like that's what it's doing. So I figure why not, I'll follow it, pass it maybe, and try to get another look at those boxes. Oh, this is important. It says Walt's Forward Trucking on the side. Anyway, I pull out behind, gaining so I can pass it, when it slows and signals a right turn, so I slow too . . . it goes toward this small warehouse. No one behind me so I just stop, try to get another good look. Here's where it gets really strange. The door goes up, and as the truck is pulling in a bunch of people come out to meet it. Not dock workers, just . . . I don't know, some people, heading toward the front of the truck. Toward the driver, you know? Then the door comes down, that's it. But I'm really curious now."

Stewart glanced at his watch, an obvious gesture for the visitor, since he had a small desk clock facing him. But all he said was "Please go on."

"Well I go home, jump on the Internet, look for Walt's Forward. I knew I saw it right, but all I could find was a post office box. That's all, nothing about the company, no ads. . . . Now I'm really into it. So I start going past that warehouse every chance I get. Nothing going on, but always several cars parked there. Saw some folks come and go around lunchtime; that was it. Meanwhile I'm not making much money, nothing but a wedding the next Saturday. I'm still looking for some shots to sell, actually found a few, but went past that warehouse a lot. Then, three days later, bingo! I see it up ahead of me, must have just left the warehouse. Daytime, busy traffic. I get up close, one car between us. I can see the boxes, one on the top back of the trailer and more on each side of the truck, the front. It gets on I-5 heading south, I'm after it. Gets up to fifty-five and stays there, right on it. So cars can go seventy, I get up to about seventy-five and get a few miles ahead. I know if it exits I'm out of the game, but I take the chance. I pick an exit, park on the ramp, run to the overpass, camera ready. Sure enough, here it comes, and I'm firing away, shooting as many as I can."

The visitor leaned forward. "Mr. Timmerlee, I can't be absolutely sure, but I think it is a remote control truck. I think those boxes might be cameras, or radar, or both, some kind of electronics. One more thing. The driver saw me as it came close, and she put her hands up on the wheel, looked at me. Of course she could have had her hands down low on the wheel and just changed position right then, but I don't know . . . I don't think so. I think the driver put her hands up to fool me. Lots of stuff about this kinda fits together, but no proof of course. The people in that warehouse middle of a Sunday night, who are they, no trucking company with that name on the road, just a mailing address, and those boxes . . . that's my guess." He leaned forward more, almost off his chair. "Mr. Timmerlee, do you know how many drivers there are in America? Do you know how many could be put out of work by driverless trucks?"

"Don't know exactly, but I'm sure it is over a million drivers."

Dorfmann nodded his head, sat back in his seat. "Yes, that's right. Maybe way over if you include all the short-haul, in-city drivers, a million-plus is close enough for the highway truckers. Frantic search for drivers all the time. I did some research, wanted to know my stuff before . . ."

The buzzer on Joe's desk sounded—Frieda on the ball, as usual. Stewart pushed a button on the intercom and said, "Another fifteen." Then to Dorfmann, "Go on. You wanted me to know about the number of drivers because . . ."

"I wanted you to take me seriously."

"Fair enough. So what did you learn?"

"It's a bitch. Sorry. It's a tough way to make a living. Bad for the ears, bad for the kidneys and who knows what else with the constant vibration, lots of loading up on meals then sitting for hours, whole lot of fat drivers, sleepy and overworked some of them, driving instead of sleeping. Good people, don't get me wrong . . . good people in a hard job. Decent money but hell to pay to get it, so after all the hours away from home and the pounding and food choices and accident risk—lots of accidents, just part of the life—the pay isn't all that wonderful, every-thing considered. You only need a high school diploma or GED and to pass driver's school and the background check, get the license, but still the haulers are always looking for drivers. Real shortage; has been for many years."

"So you think someone, some high-tech company . . ."

"Or the government. Or with them."

"Some high-tech company, maybe with government help, has decided the best answer is to put long-haul trucks out there with no drivers, just computers, GPS, cameras and such."

James Dorfmann nodded. "And save millions. Millions! Pay for the equipment, wire up the truck, never hire another diver. Cost up front, but savings enough to make it the best deal they ever saw. No drivers, no recruiting, no headaches from all the things that can go wrong when there's a human . . ."

"How about when it is raining or snowing?"

Dorfmann shrugged. "I thought about that. The only techie stuff I know is cameras, but they've come a long way in the last twenty years, amazing machines. Maybe some kind of combination camera and radar, I don't know, but I'm sure it can be done. "

Administrator Stewart Timmerlee leaned back in his elegant leather chair, put his fingertips together. After a moment he said "And put a million or more drivers out of work."

"And put a million or more drivers out of work."

A long pause, and then . . .

"Look, I've got to go, committee meeting soon. Make sure Frieda has all your contact information correct. I am interested in what you learn next."

"Sir, with all respect, I want to offer a deal."

Stewart paused. The term itself was a red flag; he had avoided scandals throughout his career and had no interest in starting now. Sitting up straight, carefully he said "What is your . . . What do you have in mind?"

"Please forgive me if this is presumptuous, but it is widely assumed you'd like to make another run at senator, be our senator. If what I think is really happening . . . is . . . then it will be a giant story, world news, anywhere there are trucks in the world—Mexico, Europe, not just the U.S. You'll have a big role in deciding how this goes down, whether or not there is a trial, national trial run; if so what does that look like, what do they have to do?"

Stewart eased back into his chair while James continued.

"Here's the deal I'm offering. Two things. First, I'll find out as much as I can, get it to you any way you tell me to, letters if you don't want an email trail. Nothing illegal, just if I pick up any more clues I let you know. I'm going to release this story right away, about a truck that may be driverless, and then ask you for a quote. Then later on there almost certainly will be a national test, a test approved by your office. When that happens let me have it first, lead photographer on the scene. You do that, and the second thing I'll do for you is write you up really good. Since I'll be the one breaking the news about the national test, I can make sure you look as good and responsible and on top of things as possible. Tell me, let me break the story, just the story that a trial is going to happen under your auspices, and I'll shine a nice light on you. That's it, that's the idea."

Stewart paused only a moment. "Probably can agree to that. Let me think on it a bit, but my preliminary answer is yes. If I do agree, yes, a letter to me." Stewart stood up, shook hands with James. "If I do agree I'll give you my home address for letters. You give me an address, I'll send you information by letter, overnight. You understand there will be no letterhead, no names or signatures, just info. I expect you would nevertheless destroy it."

"Yes to all that. A promise. Thank you, Mr. Timmerlee."

CHAPTER FOUR

James realized that he wouldn't be the only person noticing the truck with the strange attachments wheeling in and out of a Bakersfield warehouse. Everyone with a mobile phone was also everyone with a camera, and the Internet was instantaneous, worldwide. He had to get the jump on all of them, including the eastern news folks with their three-hour head start. So only two hours after his meeting with Administrator Timmerlee, from his laptop in the waiting area at Dulles International, he put together an article and sent it to Jakub Billski, James's longtime friend, a reporter for the True Post.

✳ ✳ ✳

Technology is being developed in Bakersfield, which could have a significant impact on the trucking industry by providing support for drivers. Beyond support, it may allow for driverless trucks by reducing or eliminating the need for drivers in certain situations. At this time the *Bakersfield True Post* has not been able to contact the developers. However, a truck with the equipment attached is being driven on roads and highways in our vicinity, as the picture shows. We will continue to investigate and provide information.

James R. Dorfmann, Stringer for the *Bakersfield True Post*

✳ ✳ ✳

Along with the article James sent the clearest picture he had of the truck with the words "look at top of trailer and cab" at the bottom.

The next day James got a call just passed six; he had had less than five hours of sleep and was deep under when the phone woke him. But then it hit him—it had to be the newspaper calling!

"Jakub! What's up?"

"OK so I'm not going to ask you your source, but are you sure about this? If this is right it could mean truck drivers laid off all over the country, or maybe settle for lower pay if all they do is sit in the seat and watch the truck drive by itself. Big, big shit you're dealing with here—the LCTU will explode, no doubt the politicians will weigh in, could be strikes, walkouts, hell who knows what. We print this and its wrong we have to apologize to the world."

"You're welcome, asshole. How about this? If you print it and its wrong then I never get a crack at coming on full time so I can sit around all day like you do. But what if I'm right, and I assure you I am. Two things—the *Post* scoops every paper, every radio and TV news show."

"And . . ."

"And you go to bat, hard, for me to join the family. Tell your boss it is a brilliant decision."

"Seriously, asshole yourself, if this is right I'd expect you to be invited." He paused. "Where'd you take that picture?"

"Rather not say just yet, but swear on my very balls it is authentic."

"Let's keep your nuts out of this. OK, I'm taking this up the line, telling them you're tight, got your good source."

"I understand. But if I could get it all those newshounds in Washington could find it, and don't forget they have a three-hour jump on you. If you're going to run it run it, do it now, today."

"Gotcha. Later."

"Later."

As soon as he ended the call Jakub printed the picture and took his copy of the story to the national editor, Sarah Shulman. She read it, looked up at Jakub and read it again. "I barely know Dorfmann. You buying this?"

"Sarah, come on, you know me. Think I'd bring you something I wasn't sure of? I don't waste your time."

"Sorry, yes, but this is dynamite . . . dynamite right, dynamite wrong. '. . . eliminating the need for drivers in certain situations'. . . big word, eliminating."

"There's something else." He handed over the picture. "Look at those boxes, some kind of devices on the sides, front and side of the truck and trailer." He waited while she looked carefully at the obvious, unusual additions. "Here's what James just said, just got off the phone. He said that given the reporters in D.C. being three hours ahead of us, this could be grabbed by anyone any minute. He suggested we run it next edition. I'm thinking that's too long. I'm thinking we post it now, right away on our web site. I know that's not usual, usually it's what we have in the paper. But his point is a good one; if he can find it anyone with a news nose can, and we maybe miss the scoop of the century. Run it now, run it online, then print."

Sarah took the story and picture. "I'll let you know as soon as I do. Assure me again, this guy is reliable, far as you know."

"Better yet, he wants to be a Post reporter and photographer more that he wants to breathe. Never had someone so eager to be part of our team. He punches this and it is never for him, and he knows it. I'd bet on this one, yes I would."

Sarah nodded, rose from her desk and left.

Ten minutes later Sarah came to his desk. "Call your buddy, Jakub. We're popping it on the wire in minutes. Not using the picture, not yet, have to think about when, best use. As soon as you see it call the highway safety admin, see if you can get a quote. Get the top guy if possible; name is Timmerlee, or close as you can. Maybe us knowing about the truck will open the door a little. We can tap dance a bit, pretend we know more than we do."

Jakub nodded. "What else? Anything for me to do?"

"Not yet, but soon. Right now I'll call the LCTU. I actually met the president, Drake, some years ago at an infrastructure conference in Washington. See if I can get a quote. Some other ideas . . . but call your buddy. It could be up already."

"Yes?"

"I may have to call you asshole less often. My man, we're running it. In fact, we're not waiting for the ink, we're putting it, your story, your byline, on our web page. Might be up already."

"Holy Toledo."

"Whatever that means. We're going to contact the feds, highway administration, see if we can get a quote."

A pause, then James said "I can't tell you how, but I can get you a high-level quote from them, the highway people. Let me do it."

"OK, we can run it as a follow-up, but if you don't come through quickly, sorry, we'll have to do our 'media calling' thing."

"Come through I will. Later."

"Later."

And there it was. His story, his byline, broadcast to the world. What a feeling, what a rush. James wasn't sure what to do next for the Post, and then he realized that for the first time in his journalism career he could wait, they'd come to him. Meanwhile, he had to contact Washington.

James contacted Frieda and said a short article about the truck would soon appear online from the *Bakersfield True Post*, telling her the Post is requesting Mr. Timmerlee provide a comment. Soon after James received a call. "Mr. Dorfmann, Stewart Timmerlee. I'll send you a statement in the next hour or so. Please understand that if you change one word of it that is the end of this relationship."

"Understood, absolutely."

✳ ✳ ✳

A statement from Stewart W. Timmerlee, Administrator of the National Highway Traffic Safety Administration: The National Highway Traffic Safety Administration is aware that trucks are being driven on public roads with technology that may enhance driver safety and reduce driver stress and the possibility of accidents. As further developments occur the NHTSA will provide appropriate comment.

James was disappointed; he had hoped for something that might hint at a loss of jobs, as his article had. But he kept his word and forwarded it to Jakub, with a firm warning to not change one word, that doing so would eliminate an important pipeline to the federal government.

CHAPTER FIVE

Several members of the staff of the Lorry, Carriage, and Truckers Union, the LCTU, had their computers set to Google search the internet for news about unions, the trucking and airline industries, public service, and all the other occupations with LCTU members, especially any Congressional discussions or news conferences that referenced their members' world of work. Lots of hits, but the searches were split among many of the staff and they all became adroit at glancing at the hits as they popped up and deleting, occasionally passing them to the appropriate staff member or, in certain situations, forwarding them marked URGENT to the President, Simon Drake. The story from the *Bakersfield True Post* certainly met the latter qualification.

In Washington, Simon Drake was in a staff meeting when his secretary, Doris Rosen, came in and told him he had an urgent phone call from California, that something of enormous consequence was about to break on the internet. He rose to go to his office, asking as he did so who was calling. The response was the National Editor of the *Bakersfield True Post*, a woman named Shulman. He frowned a moment, then vaguely remembered her from a meeting some time ago.

"This is Simon Drake."

"Simon, Sarah Shulman here from the *Bakersfield True Post*. I hope you remember me from a conference we attended about two years ago."

"Impossible to forget, Sarah . . . brilliant and lovely."

"I'll tell my grandchildren you said so. Simon, I'm calling because just minutes ago we popped something on our web site you have got to see. I want a quote, but if you need some time to digest it we can talk again in a bit. But please give me something from the LCTU."

"Call you back at this number I see?"

"Yes, direct to me."

"Got to talk to my folks, but three hours tops, likely sooner, I promise."

Simon wrote her phone number down, sat at his desk, and found the site and the story. He read it, stared and read it again. He then called in his secretary and asked her to put it on the screen in the conference room. Simon returned, the meeting still in progress, saying "Sorry, we have to suspend this. Take a look," he said, gesturing toward the screen. Nothing happened for a long thirty seconds, then the projector came to life and James Dorfmann's story was on the screen. Simon sat down heavily and waited while the others read the story. Stunned silence.

Even in an era in America where union membership and political clout were lower than almost any time since the 1950s, Simon Drake was successful at building a strong union, the LCTU. He did this by leaving his D.C. office often, visiting union halls across the country, sometimes away from the office for a week or more as he moved from state to state. He assembled a competent, loyal team and trusted them to run things well while he was gone, which they did, and he trusted their advice. After giving them moments to consider the news story, Simon turned to them and said, "I want to get something out right away. Call my contact at the paper and give her a good quote. Brainstorm time. Chuck, will you do the whiteboard honors, please? Punishment for having a nice handwriting."

They knew each other well, trusted their instincts. In good brainstorming fashion they started by just throwing out phrases, points to be made, possible conclusions. The winnowing and assembling process took only about an hour. He returned the call to Sarah Shulman ninety minutes after she called him, told her the quote was coming to her email address.

A statement from Simon Drake, President, Lorry, Carriage, and Truckers Union:

The LCTU has read with interest the *Bakersfield True Post* article regarding a truck with electronic capabilities. Those capabilities allow the technology to take over some portion of the responsibilities now those of America's skilled long-haul drivers. While the LCTU cannot comment further on the technology until more information is available, we are of course concerned that the safety of our drivers and their trucks and loads, and certainly the safety of everyone who shares the highways with those trucks, might be compromised. LCTU drivers are careful, committed, and always safety-conscious, and while technology that would enhance and support that dedication to safety would be welcome, it must be demonstrated that it would be an enhancement and not a distraction to our dedicated, professional drivers.

CHAPTER SIX

Josiah (Joe) Williams started his career as an officer in the Detroit Police Department after earning a bachelor's degree in social work with a minor in criminology. In his eighth year, thirty years old, he was wounded by a man who then committed suicide. Joe could no longer stand for any length of time, couldn't run, so he was assigned a desk job. It was acceptable, he even got a promotion, but it didn't satisfy him. Believing his dream of becoming a deputy chief or higher now gone, he looked for something else to fill his life.

He found it as a member of the Detroit City Council, where he served while working nearly full time in a desk job for the police force; busy, productive years. That led to his election as mayor, whereupon he took early retirement and concentrated on serving the city in that capacity, working to resolve the city's economic challenges. His success as mayor led to election to the United States House of Representatives. Joe's support comes from police and firefighters and hourly workers in his district; although only eighteen percent of employees are unionized there, they are strong supporters who vote and get out the vote. Josiah Williams is a good union man.

The morning after the article appeared Simon Drake called and asked to see Representative Williams as soon as possible. With the union headquarters only six blocks away they were able to agree on a time later that day. He was greeted warmly, then they got right to it, no small talk.

"Joe, if this stuff really works it is a disaster for us, for the LCTU. I'm not an electrical whiz, but I know enough about radar and GPS and cameras to know that a truck could be driven without a human. Hell's bells, cars were equipped to do it ten years ago! I'm not saying it can't happen, although some of our folks, some staff members are saying it isn't possible, always need a driver. Wish they were right, but fact is they're wrong. A truck could be driven from coast to coast without a human, only to pump diesel, that's it. I didn't get to be president of a union with almost a million and a half members by not keeping up with things or denying reality. This is real. It's pure shit, but it's real."

"And so we're meeting . . .

"You're a representative with a great reputation, people respect you, and you're a union man from way back. I thought you'd listen, be interested."

"You're assuming I'd take the union's side if Congress takes it up. Good guess."

"I want you to put a bill in the hopper, now, saying there has to be a driver in any truck on interstate highways. No driverless trucks."

Ten days later Representative Josiah Williams proposed House Bill one one four. A few days later he rose to speak in support of it.

"Madam Speaker, I wish to speak on behalf of house bill one one four. Madam Speaker, America's truck drivers, hard-working men and women, are the backbone of our transportation system. They are responsible for delivering the goods that help make this country great; food, clothing, furniture, electronics, making those deliveries while they and their employers obey a myriad of regulations. America's trucks are the safest in the world because of those professional, careful drivers and the regulations they follow, because of the requirements for inspections and logs, and also because of the fine troopers, men and women, who patrol our nation's highways. What recent events have disclosed is a move to replace these important, key players in America's commerce with electronics, giant robots on wheels, spinning down the highway at sixty miles an hour or more with no human control. We have before us a grave situation, one where an electronics firm would assist trucking companies to end the employment of a million or more drivers. Let me repeat that number, Madam Speaker. Over one million drivers, earning seventy billion a year or more, removed from our economy. If this electronic travesty is allowed what will we have? We will have seventy billion dollars of paychecks not earned, not being spent, each and every year. That alone is cause to pull back from this dangerous concept. But it is on top of the idea of driverless trucks, fully loaded weighing up to forty tons—forty tons, Madam Speaker—careening down our roads filled with citizens in their family cars, and no human to foresee danger or think with the skills, the experience, the wisdom of our fine drivers with their years of exposure to all kinds of road and traffic situations. This is a recipe for disaster, for slaughter on our highways. House Bill one one four will prevent that slaughter by assuring that there is always a licensed driver, a properly trained driver with a Commercial Driver's License, a CDL, behind the wheel. Thank you."

The day after Representative Williams' speech Walt stepped into Frank's office at the warehouse. Frank was spending more time there, almost thirty hours a week, plus thirty or so with his investment firm, a schedule sure to hold until the day, when that day comes, that the NHTSA approved his trucks for public roads.

"Well, it happened, a Congressional warning against our evil invention. 'Careening down our roads,' family cars at risk . . . "

"Could have been worse. He didn't call us evil, just warned about our trucks. What the hell, we all knew this day was coming, and . . . well, I said, it could have been worse."

Walt gestured toward the two computers on Frank's desk. "Whatcha working on?"

"I remember something I heard, I don't know, business class or maybe read it . . . not important. Anyway, the thing goes something like this, about how to start a small business. Doesn't matter what kind, restaurant or investment house or furniture store, rule applies. It's about budgeting to get going, get it off the ground first day. Here's what you do; figure everything, staff of course, something for your pocket so you won't starve, rent or buy space—probably rent—furniture, equipment, tools you need. A restaurant, stoves and refrigerators and napkins, all that. An investment house like mine, computers, and a techie to honcho them, and comfortable chairs and pens and paper. Whatever business, figure everything you'll need. Everything, put a number on it, dollars. Total that up. And then . . . ? Frank's hands did a drum roll on the desk. "Double it. Double that final number, and when you've got that in hand, or for sure can get it when you need it, that's when you open your doors."

Walt smiled. "So you did that for this, I'm guessing. How's the formula holding?

"Pretty good. We're spending a little more than I planned, but not bad, no reason to sweat, not yet. So . . . about the speech. Bull by the horns. I'm going to contact the worthy representative, ask for a meeting. His office, his turf. Beard the lion in his den."

"Haven't heard that one since high school. So . . . how soon?"

"Going to crunch some numbers here a bit longer, then call. We'll see."

"I'll leave you to your crunching and calling. Oh, some good news. Found a local shop to give us a good price on the broadcast camera for the trailer. Need to get a pickup in the computer, accept the signal, but not a big deal."

"Good, thanks."

Frank contacted Representative Josiah Williams's office, asked for a meeting as soon as possible. He was given a date in ten days; that seemed like a deliberate negative gesture but he decided to accept it with grace—actually he realized he had no choice but to do so.

The Representative's office was one of the less ornate in Congress; Josiah felt that he wanted his visitors to feel comfortable, whatever their personal situation. He had four items on his walls; he did not display his college degree, but a small plaque of appreciation from the Detroit Police Department, a map of Michigan, a map of the Greater Detroit area, and a picture of his modest boyhood home. On his credenza were family pictures.

When Frank Stevenson arrived he was quickly admitted to the Representative's office. They shook hands politely, and Frank was invited to take a seat in one of the four comfortable armchairs facing the desk. Josiah stayed behind the desk.

"Representative Williams, thank you for giving me this opportunity to meet. I've read your proposed bill HB one one four, and your speech in support of it. I fully understand your concern, and the concern of those you speak for and represent. My response, if I may."

"I assumed you came twenty-six hundred miles to do just that, give that response. I try very hard to be informed, to try to see all sides of issues, but, as you said, there are those I represent. So please—go ahead."

"Let me start with what no doubt will sound harsh. We, my engineers and technical people and I, believe a robotic vehicle can be designed that can be safer than any human. That is, the cameras, GPS, software, can think faster, make decisions quicker, than a human. It just does. But we don't see all truck drivers losing their jobs, certainly not soon. First of all...."

Josiah interrupted him. "If you're going to give me a list of reasons why your technology can safely replace a human, I need that list. I'm fine with listening now, but can you also send them to me right away in an email so I can study, think about them? You have my office email, right?"

"Yes, and I'll be glad to send them right away. So thanks for letting me do it this way."

"Not at all."

Frank sat back a bit, relaxing imperceptibly. This was familiar territory. "The technology is being tested repeatedly in all kinds of conditions. The computer system samples the situation, the input from all cameras and GPS, twenty times a second. That's way slow in computer time, nothing like the million or more possible, but plenty for our purposes. That information is being fed back to a central source, a secure site, where several trucks—we haven't decided on the number yet—are monitored by a human, whom we call a wrangler. If something is happening that the computer doesn't understand the human can take control faster than an eyeblink. But let me be clear about this . . . the truck drives, safely at the speed limit in the right lane, aware of everything around it. It reads speed limits, detour signs, signals from police or highway patrol. It moves over a lane when it sees emergency or police vehicles on the shoulder. In short, it is a careful, lawful, respectful driver."

"How often will the wrangler control it? And how?"

"Excellent questions, sir. In normal driving conditions, never. Never. The system—we call it T O T, short for truck operation technology—the system reads traffic lights of course, can get from a warehouse to, say, a port dock with no human assistance. The situation is not that T O T needs help driving, not at all. However, there might be some extreme situation where the computer doesn't know what to do. As I said, it reads detour signs, turns on wipers on the cameras in the rain, turns on lights as needed . . . so we don't think the wranglers will be involved often, which is why we're still not sure how many trucks one wrangler can be responsible for, but it might be eight or ten or more, still to be decided. To answer your second question . . . there is a mockup of the cab of the truck, with a steering wheel, pedals, gearshift. The mockup can display each individual truck; for instance if it is an automatic gearshift or an old fashioned one with a clutch, that's what the wrangler will see, have. The wrangler can then, quite literally, drive the truck; the feel of the wheel and the pedals is exactly what a person in the cab would feel. If you've ever wondered what it would be like to drive an eighteen wheeler loaded with several tons of cargo, please visit, we'll put you behind that wheel, you'll swear you were booming down the highway in the real thing."

"I'll sure take you up on that. But what about drivers out of work? A million? Come on, that's a hell of a hit to the economy, to hundreds of thousands of families . . . I don't see how I can not fight for a driver in each truck, driving or not."

"Sir, I'm certainly not going to tell you how Congress works, but my, our guess is that once the highway commission approves T O T, and we're certain that day is coming, that the trucking industry will prevail in phasing out drivers over time. Maybe a long time, but eventually phasing out most of them, at least long-haul drivers. Sir, a driver just isn't needed to drive on I-Seventy from Pittsburgh to Topeka. Just not needed."

Josiah Williams sat a long moment, Frank Stevenson waited. "Thank you for coming all this way, three time zones. Much appreciated. I've got some heavy thinking to do. Please send the list soon, the more detail the better."

"I will. And thank you for seeing me."

CHAPTER SEVEN

Ellen Michel climbed into GeeCee in the Bakersfield warehouse and well-concealed laboratory. She started the engine and leaned against her new back support, a plastic pillow with air puffed into it. The truck was full; not only the usual computers but cameras too, one pointed at her, one at the top of the gearshift, one at the floor capturing her feet and the pedals. The truck started to roll, heading west for its big test; a dress rehearsal before going public.

It was six a.m. The only person who might have noticed the truck, even followed it, wasn't there. James R. Dorfmann was just waking up, and the truck would be well on its way before he made one of his two or three daily passes in front of the warehouse, hoping to see something, hoping to see that strange truck again.

GeeCee entered I-5 south of the city, went north then shortly after four hours took 80 heading north and east.

It was now four hours since departure, and as planned GeeCee pulled into a large truck stop, finding a parking spot but stopping a bit off angle from the other trucks. Ellen immediately heard a voice from the radio "Ellen, take control, back up a bit and bring her more lined up with the other trucks. We'll run this through our software, see what the glitch is."

"Easy for you to say. I'm going to eat breakfast with a bunch of guys making wise cracks about women drivers."

Despite her concern no one commented on the parking adjustment. But when she came out of the truck stop there were two drivers walking around GeeCee, pointing. "Yours?"

"Yep."

"So what are those things?"

Ellen answered as Walt had rehearsed her, saying they had to do something with safety, some experiment; she sure didn't understand it.

"Bet its something some government asshole came up with, doesn't know a damn thing about driving but wants to add more stuff for us to pay attention to. Dumb."

"Yep, could be" Ellen answered, then got in the truck and started it up. She was careful to put her hands on the wheel and gearshift, but the truckers weren't watching her, and she relaxed as she left the parking lot.

After breakfast the trip continued. Near Colfax a light rain started to fall. This had been predicted and anticipated, an important part of the test. Ellen watched carefully, her right hand on her leg, less than a second's reach from the toggle switch that would give her control. But GeeCee just turned on the headlights and continued at a constant speed, right at the speed limit. Back in the Bakersfield lab the engineers and programmers and Walt and Frank watched the monitors. Suddenly the rain picked up, doubling then doubling again; the skies opened up in a torrential downpour. This was not in the weather prediction. The tension in the lab picked up and Ellen moved her hand to three inches from the toggle, her left hand poised above the wheel.

GeeCee did what the software code writers and programmers designed and installed. The diesel slowed, downshifting, dropping to 50, then 45, holding there. The fog lights came on and the wipers—windshield and on the cameras—went from intermittent to full speed. The heavy rain lasted about five minutes, then GeeCee started to emerge from the storm, driving straight and true, moving back up to the speed limit, turning off the headlights and, after a few moments, the wipers. Ellen sat back, again put her hands in her lap. "Nice work, GeeCee. I think you drive 'bout as good as I do."

For the first time Ellen spoke toward the microphone mounted just past the steering wheel. "So, so here's a problem. Of course only a problem if there is a human behind the wheel, if not ain't no thing . . . We're through the rain, sunny, wipers stopped, but there is still spray coming from the road, you know, passing trucks and cars, plus some coming off the hood . . . anyway, only thing I can think to do is take control so I can run the wipers. Shouldn't there be some way I can work them on my own? And the washer fluid, shouldn't I control that someway without taking the whole truck, you know, flipping the big switch?" The engineers leaned toward each other, agreed they missed one, solution being a new toggle to override just the washer/wiper system.

Walt responded. "Absolutely right, Ellen, thanks much, we're on it."

GeeCee continued on 80, now in bright sunshine, over the state line and through Reno, then soon after left the interstate at Fernley, taking 50 southeast to Fallon.

While continuing to monitor the cameras and radar and gauges the staff gave each other high fives, smiles, friendly banter between the hardware and software designers and builders; with the exception of the concern Ellen raised the test went almost perfectly. A slight parking error, that was it, but driving on the interstate in heavy rain, driving on a state route, going into a parking lot with moving vehicles and finding a place to park, then pulling out and onto the road, all perfection. GeeCee was ready. T O T was splendid. Drivers were expendable.

As GeeCee and Ellen headed home, Frank tipped his head toward Walt, quietly indicating he wanted Walt to follow him to the next room. "Walt, I don't want to wait until she gets back to call the feds and ask for a sanctioned test. I'm going to call right now, see if I can get a meeting with someone as high up in the highway administration as possible— hell, I'm going to try for the top. I think all I have to do is take some video, especially that piece when she went through the heavy rain, and maybe when we take her off the interstate and go into a small town, park at a truck stop. If something craps out I'll have to cancel, that will make it harder maybe to get in the door next time, but I'm willing to run the risk. I want us to be running that national test now, as soon as we can. Don't know who is watching us, who took pictures . . . time's a'wasting, ain't it?"

"You're gambling nothing will go wrong."

"I'm gambling nothing will go wrong. If nothing does, I'll ask for one half hour, play twenty-nine minutes of video and shake hands. That's my plan."

CHAPTER EIGHT

The Club is not actually a club but rather a fine D.C. restaurant open to the public, with a general dining room but also numerous private rooms for conversations of groups as large as twenty or as small as two. The food is excellent, even exquisite, the ambiance all dark wood and leather and white cloth tabletops, the service impeccable, the prices high.

Robert Banage is a lobbyist for the Fabricators, Manufacturers and Assemblers United Front. The FMAUF is a powerful lobbying organization pushing for legislation that benefits its members and supports their production capability and profit making as much as possible, also advocating for tariffs and restrictions that limit foreign competition. They have millions of dollars to donate to the campaign coffers of members of Congress who support their agenda, and do so every election. The results, in terms of friendly legislation, encourage the member firms to continue providing funding.

When Josiah Williams received a lunch invitation from Robert Banage he knew immediately it would be about House Bill one one four, but he had been wooed and warned at The Club and similar restaurants before, part of being a member of Congress, so he had no reservation about accepting the invitation. He would insist on paying for his meal.

Banage had reserved one of the two-person rooms, was there first, and greeted the representative warmly. The waiter—in the restaurant's uniform of black slacks, dark blue shirt, white tie and black and blue checked vest—took their drink orders. Both choose a glass of Malbec. The waiter left, gently closing the door.

"Let me guess, Bob. Your shop isn't happy about one one four."

"Short answer, yes, correct. Reasons, if I may."

"Sure, of course."

"Let's start with the technology. We have no interest in putting trucks on the road that aren't safe, certainly not. But the technology is, well, awesome. Whatever questions you have let me know; either the manufacturers or I will answer promptly. Further, you say what test you want a truck to pass, you design it, and we'll make it happen. We anticipate a national approval test, a test by the highway administration, and you can help design it. We want . . ."

"Sorry to interrupt. . . . "

"No, that's fine. What?"

"You said the manufacturers will answer my questions. Your organization doesn't own the trucks, doesn't own the technology, the system. How can you make that promise?"

I met with the designers, company named MHR, got a tour. I showed up with a lot of questions, some of them no doubt the same ones you'd ask. We were together almost four hours, I learned a ton."

"Did you tell them what you, actually the FMAUF, thought of the technology?"

"Yes. After I reported back to our people we let MHR know that we are supportive of their installing the systems when they're ready and tested, and federally approved, nationwide. We know that means— eventually—a great reduction in the number of drivers behind wheels, but that takes place gradually, over years, many years . . . but happens it does. However, none of that takes place until the feds approve the technology. So again, you say what you want to be included in the national test, I have no doubt the feds and the manufacturers will comply. I mean it. Pouring rain, dark night, crowded highway, detour, road under repair, highway patrol giving directions, anything. Even highway patrol using a flashlight to direct traffic on a moonless night in the middle of nowhere. You name the challenge . . . no, challenges, and we'll do the demonstrations. Josiah, the technology is amazing. You know, look at all the things we take for granted now, every day. We carry a metal package in our pockets that can let us talk to anyone anywhere in the world, plus find our way through a strange city, plus calculate our taxes, plus…"

"I get it, I get it. We take our phones, which are far more than phones, for granted. And TV remotes. And the televisions themselves. And computers in our cars. Point taken, but you're still talking about tons of metal at sixty miles an hour, or more, with no human in control."

"Important note, the truck doesn't go faster than the speed limit. Ever. But back to my offer…. you, or members of your team, or others, design the tests. Make them as challenging as possible. That's fine. As for humans, let me tell you about the wranglers."

"Wranglers?"

"The trucks can handle about ninety-eight, maybe ninety-nine percent of the situations they would confront. But if the truck encounters something the computer isn't sure about, not sure what to do, it carefully slows, puts on warning blinkers, and notifies a human, a wrangler, that's what they call them. That person sees everything the truck sees, all the cameras, the GPS, everything. The wrangler can then actually drive the truck sitting in a full-scale mockup of the truck cab. I have to tell you, it is mind-blowing. Test them, please. But here's the point … "

The waiter appeared with their wine, took their orders—a burger and fries for Robert, a Caesar salad with shrimp for Josiah—and left.

"I don't want to sound callous or cruel. I know I'm talking about tens of thousands of honest, decent, middle Americans driving those trucks, all of them losing their jobs, their income. I know it; we know it. But the reality is that the time has come for driverless trucks." He leaned forward, just a little. A posture of emphasis, but not aggressive. "The time has come for driverless trucks. Look, we don't make buggy whips anymore, nor buggies for that matter, except a very few for a small group of people. We sure don't make television tubes anymore. We don't make vacuum tubes for radios or television. Time and science and technology march on, Josiah, they just do. They just do." Robert

GEECE

leaned back, his posture easing. He knew it was important to let people think when he delivered a message; knowing when to stop talking was a critical skill in his profession.

"And voters vote. Damn it; let's stop playing games. You want me to drop my bill or at least water it way down, or you won't provide any funding for my next campaign. Or better, you'll fund an opposition candidate."

"I never said . . ."

"Stuff it. Again, let's stop playing games. The problem is that my voters are as Middle America, even lower Middle America, as it gets. If I'm seen as going back on my dedication to protect trucker jobs, jobs my voters are sure familiar with, I'll be out on my ass. I could write my opponents speech for him, or her, so easily. All about selling out to corporate interests and turning my back on the common man or woman and being anti-family and lunching with lobbyists in private rooms in swanky restaurants. Sorry, I really like being a representative, and by the way I'm damn good at it, on the case for my constituents."

"Yes, yes you are. But we're going to get behind any member of Congress who supports us. So." A brief pause. "So in addition to the offer to have you challenge the technology, give us tests to pass, let's talk about every place except America." Again the gentle forward lean, the positive posture. "We don't know yet how soon the technology pays for itself, how soon adding all those cameras and whatnot but eliminating the driver gets to black ink, but we know it does. The techies, if you'll meet with them, can give you a good guess, but at some point costs go down. It's like solar panels on a house roof; at some point the savings in electric bills equals the cost of installation, and from then on it is all good. If we don't do this, driverless trucks, our competitors in Canada, Mexico, Europe will. If it is only something found in this country, or another country, it won't make any difference of course; German beer hauled around Europe might be cheaper with those trucks, but we don't make that here, so no advantage except the import price might drop a bit. But anything made here and elsewhere that depends on trucking will give that elsewhere an advantage. Car parts. Motorcycles. Sporting goods. Clothing.

Appliances. Toys. Everything on that list, and more, are made in the good old USA but also in other countries, and if they can cut costs . . . well, you get it, sorry for the basic econ lecture."

The waiter returned with their meals, refilled the water glasses, quietly left. Both men spent some moments eating; Robert again using silence as a friend, letting his words work, letting Josiah think.

"This isn't simple, Bob. Tell you what, let me think about that test idea, the invitation, come up with something. Then maybe I can . . . no, never mind, that's beside the point. It is either drivers yes or drivers no, can't be slightly pregnant, right? I stand behind the bill or I don't. I push for a driver in the cab or I don't." Josiah paused, Robert waited. "Hell, I'm sure the trucks can become everything you're pushing, safe, cost effective, the next big science breakthrough. Gift to humanity, but with dead jobs. I've got to think really hard about this, do some discreet polling, talk to my advisors."

"Sure. Let me know about the tests. I'd say no rush, but we really should have your answer in about ninety days so we know which way to go with our campaign funding. So please describe a test as soon as possible, and how about ninety days from today for your decision, OK?"

"That'll work. Can we talk sports now?"

"Which team you want to praise or trash?"

Five days later Representative Williams called Robert Banage. "Bob? Josiah. Listen, I've got an idea, a test request."

"Do it."

"Dark of night, small road, middle of nowhere, barrier with road closed signs. Reflective, that's all right, but no lights, nothing. The truck stops at, near, the barrier. Then a police officer, maybe highway patrol, emerges from the dark, moves the barrier, waves the truck through with a flashlight. And . . . a water truck, water tank, so a hose, no, make that two garden hoses, sprayed at the windshield and all the electronics. Not ridiculous, just mimicking a heavy rain. That's it."

"Done. Thank you."

CHAPTER NINE

Representative Josiah Williams accepted the invitation to visit the Bakersfield T O T development facility, partly to be fully informed, but also to spend time in a technology setting, something he rarely got to do; lots of boardroom discussions, but he really liked walking the factory floor, seeing those amazing machines and skilled employees turning out products. He also planned on a few vacation days visiting the northern California wine country. Wanting to appear less Congressperson and more interested third party, he left his suit in his hotel room, instead wearing casual slacks and a comfortable shirt. When he arrived at the warehouse he was pleased to see that others were similarly dressed and that he had made the right decision.

Frank introduced Representative Williams, who quickly said, "Just call me Joe" to Walt and Ellen. After brief conversations and a tour the visitor was taken to the wrangler's setup, referred to by the engineers as 'the situation room.' At that point Frank made an offer.

"If you would like to, you can sit in the wrangler's chair, see what it's like. You could also drive a truck that's out on the highway from here, actually be in control."

"Thank you, I think I'd like that, but what if I mess up? I've never driven something that large before."

"Here's what we're proposing. Ellen, our test driver, will take GeeCee out on the highway. At that point you'll be able to drive the truck, so pretty much straight, open highway, a few curves, but no city traffic. T O T will hold it at fifty-five, so you won't have to shift or adjust the speed, just steer."

"Sure, let's do that."

"We thought that might be your answer, so after you met her Ellen took GeeCee out, she's almost on the highway right now. Have a seat," Frank said, indicating the driver's seat in the mockup cab.

There was nothing in front of Joe except a large blank screen. The engineers pushed a few buttons and suddenly Joe was behind the wheel of a tractor pulling a trailer, an eighteen wheeler in the right lane of a highway, speedometer stuck at fifty-five. His eyes widened. At the top of the screen was a view from the back of the trailer. To either side were mirrors showing the sides of the trailer and some distance behind the truck.

"How did you do that, how do you show me what I'd see in the mirrors?"

"Just behind the doors to the cab, almost at the back of the cab, the tractor, are cameras aimed at the mirrors. They are the most expensive cameras, and actually caused us to adjust our starting price a bit, raise it. What we realized is that in a strong rain or snowstorm the cameras, facing forward, would be useless. So they actually have miniature windshield wipers that go back and forth, fairly rapidly, on the lens. And small heater coils, too. Of course they are only needed when a wrangler takes over, otherwise the mirrors aren't necessary, GeeCee knows what's all around her. The mirrors are only for human eyes, if needed, same with those cameras. Still, had to have them."

"Interesting. Far-sighted. I'm getting the impression you thought of everything."

"Sure do hope so, Joe. This is a great staff, smart engineers and software designers, but Ellen has been so valuable too, bringing her real world, real driver point of view to us. So, ready to drive?"

"Yes. So…. Ellen will take over if I need help?"

"Actually, she'll flip a switch to take control from you and give it to GeeCee. That's exactly what would happen if a wrangler drove for a while, then was no longer needed."

"Let's do it!"

"OK, put your hands on the wheel, you'll have control in a moment. GeeCee is holding at the truck speed limit, fifty-five, so all you'll have to do is steer." Frank leaned forward, spoke into a microphone. "Flip it off, Ellen. Thanks."

Joe suddenly felt the steering wheel come alive in his hands. He concentrated on keeping the truck centered in the right lane. After a few moments he glanced at the top of the screen, saw a car coming up on the trailer, moving to the passing lane. The car then appeared in his left mirror; there were no blind spots, the passing car was visible from some distance behind the trailer, through the pass, and then pulling ahead and back into the right lane. Up ahead was a long, gentle curve to the right. In the cab Ellen moved her hand close to the ON switch, but the visitor guided the truck smoothly through the curve.

"OK, that's enough. Someone else drive."

Frank chuckled, told Ellen to turn T O T back on; the engineers would tell GeeCee to come home.

"Frank, I'm sweating. Haven't been that nervous in a long, long time."

"In all fairness, Joe, other drivers go through driving school, pass a test, get a CDL. You jumped behind the wheel at fifty-five. A little sweat is understandable."

CHAPTER TEN

Lobbyist Robert Banage realized he had made a promise, a reasonable one, but one that had to be kept to bring Josiah Williams toward his point of view, moving him away from the 'always a driver in the cab' position. He called Frank Stevenson.

"Mr. Stevenson, Robert Banage.

"Hello. I thought we were doing first names."

"Yes, sorry, force of habit, lobbyist politeness. . . . Good to talk to you again. I met with Representative Josiah Williams. I'm sure you know his position on driverless trucks."

"Oh yes, completely."

"The FMAUF is supportive of what you're doing, makes good economic sense. But I'm telling you what you know. Here's the situation; I went out on a limb, made a promise only you can keep. My apologies if I've created a problem, but, well, I got a little carried away trying to sway the good Congressman."

"Promise being . . ."

"I told him that if there were to be, sorry, that when there will be a national test, the highway administration involved, that he could design part of that test."

"And he suggested drive across the ocean. Or to the North Pole. Sorry, go ahead."

"Some lost and gone country road, night… he didn't say moonless, but I'm guessing that's what he had in mind. So there's a road closed sign, maybe on a sawhorse or something similar. Truck stops, then a cop appears and moves the sawhorse, gives the go-ahead with a flashlight. The truck proceeds."

"So far, piece of cake. That's it?"

"Rain. Park a water truck nearby, two hoses spraying water in the air, enough that it duplicates a pretty good storm."

"And . . . ?"

"That's it."

"You can climb off that limb. All except the cop with flashlight we've got it; tested many times, rain and small roads and night. As for the human giving directions through hand or flashlight signals, two answers. First, we have set up that situation a few times, mixed results, still working on it. But the better answer is that this is a classic situation where the person in the home warehouse, the wrangler, would receive an alert, would be, quite literally, asked by GeeCee for help. T O T might be able to handle it, might not, but that's what the wranglers are for. Between now and any national test we'll have more time to work on that human-signal recognition software, really not that technically challenging."

Frank Stevenson requested a one-hour meeting with Stewart Timmerlee. Because of Frank's position as head of a successful investment firm, known for helping people and firms grow wealth—often impressive growth —with no hint of scandal, Stewart was interested in meeting him. He wondered what MHR Investors had for the highway administration, perhaps a new safety device. Frieda Shippens scheduled a meeting eight days later, and made it at 11:00 in case they wanted time to continue talking over lunch.

Frank came in with a laptop computer. After a brief introduction he got right to it.

"Please watch this. I'll be glad to answer any questions, but I think it best if we begin with the video."

He turned the screen toward Stewart and pressed enter. A split screen appeared; one a view of a driver behind the wheel of a truck in a typical truck cab, the other a view from low facing forward, perhaps just above the bumper. The truck started to move, evidenced by the landscape moving past the driver—a woman, Stewart noticed—and the front view. Although he knew about the development of a driverless truck, starting with his meeting with James Dorfmann, and had issued a neutral statement for the press, still Stewart's eyes went wide as he realized the driver wasn't moving. At the bottom of the screen was telemetry showing speed, gear selected and total miles for the trick. Stewart could not take his eyes from the screen; it was almost like a movie with great special effects, except he knew it was true, had happened. The driver never moved except to scratch her nose. In various scenes the truck turned, stopped at red lights and stop signs, entered the interstate and held the speed limit, moved to the left to give room around a highway patrol car, the trooper talking to the stopped driver. Finally it pulled into a garage through what looked like a warehouse door and stopped. The driver had not once touched the wheel.

The video lasted about thirty minutes. When it was over Stewart looked up. "I don't know what to say. I'm assuming this is all real, no tricks. And I noticed a piece was missing."

"I assure you sir, no tricks. Yes, we cut out a portion where the truck was driving on an interstate with no change in speed, no challenges, lots of drivers passing us. The test was about one hundred miles and I didn't want to bore you, nothing to see but a right-lane view, mile after mile. If you'd like I can send you the original, and you can have any experts look at the tape. I assure you, sir, it is just what you are seeing, no tricks, no special anything. We have developed a truly safe, totally safe, driverless truck. We're using technology that has existed for over ten years, just put it together and took it up a level. While impressive, it really isn't that hard to do, in terms of software and hardware."

"I can understand servers controlling the brakes and fuel supply, doing what those pedals would do, and the gear selection is built into the automatic transmission, but how do you control steering?"

"That was a bit tricky. We had to add motors to replace the arms of the driver, find room for them. Tricky, but not impossible."

"Wow. Very, very impressive. So what's next, and how can this office help you?"

"We want a national test, a sanctioned test. We want to drive from a location in California, our lab in Bakersfield, mostly but not all interstate. We're asking the NHTSA to observe it with cameras . . . or any way that would satisfy your administration. The goal would be to have approval, officially, that these trucks are legal on the interstates. We want your blessing, in other words. We'll take care of all costs, including security."

"Security?"

"Mister Timmerlee, this will eventually put hundreds of thousands of long-haul drivers out of work, no doubt about it. Even if Congress passes a law saying there has to be a driver sitting in the seat, something we think might happen, we're sure those will be lower paying positions, lower hourly or maybe even salaried. Salaried, with benefits, but probably half to two thirds of present earnings." He paused. "However, we absolutely believe that for most long-haul routes no driver is needed, just a redundant person sitting there, watching. But that's a battle. . . sorry, conversation for your administration, Congress, the LCTU, the public to have. Whether there will be a person sitting in the cab or not isn't up to us."

"But you believe, based on, I guess, tests like you just showed me, that the reality is drivers, some drivers, could be eliminated. That's . . . significant, for sure."

"We know they can be eliminated. But as I said, not up to us."

"Lower costs to shippers, I'm assuming even after installing your system."

"Of course a lot depends on the level of wages if there have to be drivers sitting in the cabs, but we figure—given lower wages—a per-tractor break-even of under ten years. After that the savings pile up, obviously much quicker if there is no human in the cab; break-even point under five years. Our guess is it will be a few companies going without drivers, and they'll offer lower shipping rates to grab business, then more and more. The drivers are no doubt going to protest.

The LCTU is going to scream bloody murder. You of course know about House Bill one one four. Don't know what will happen with that, but we think there may be a law requiring a seat in the seat for at least some years. However…we can put forth a case that if drivers are required, but at a lower wage, it still is a financial win for any firm that installs the equipment."

Stewart leaned back in his large, dark-brown leather chair. "So maybe massive layoffs at some point in the future, maybe not. But if there are drivers it won't be the decent earnings they have now."

"No it won't, but, well I said it, that's for the owners and operators and LCTU and Congress to work out." Frank paused. "Here's another way of looking at it. As I said, the technology is over a decade old. And although we've laid on every patent we can think of, we don't doubt a competitor will show up with a similar system. After all, it is just feed-back; the camera sees X, the software says when you see X do Y. Lots of software code, lots of expensive techies with their faces in computers, but really not that much of a challenge, not awesome science. We will be lowering the price as soon as possible to ward off challengers, but someone will emerge. And we want to sell our patents in seven to ten years, cash out, go find the next big idea."

"You're not an engineering firm, but you took this on, rather than backing one as an investment, classic venture capital play. My I ask why?"

"An engineer came to us with the idea. We talked about a lot of options, eventually decided to bring him on board, let him build a team, give him money to work with. He understands that if it doesn't work, he walks away with only the salary he's been paid. If it works he'll be rich. Very rich. And we believe we'll be able to sell and get out for a nice number."

"Want to go to lunch? Sorry, has to be separate checks."

"Sure."

"You can leave your computer here. I assure you it will be safe."

"Please don't be offended, I believe you, but we've got too many dollars tied up in this. I'll carry it, if you don't mind."

Stewart W. Timmerlee shrugged. "Not at all. Not at all."

They walked to a restaurant three blocks away, Aaliyah's Is A Fish House. They both ordered a half-dozen oysters as an appetizer, then continued their conversation.

"Frank, how do you envision this national test? I know you said a California starting point."

"We figure close to twenty hours, so two days of movement, ten hours each, plus about an hour each day at the most for food, otherwise rolling unless she has to pee and can't wait."

"*She?*"

"Hell of a woman. More about her in a minute."

The waiter appeared with the oysters. The two men took a minute to prepare them to taste, choosing from the mignonette sauce and lemon.

Frank continued. "Right now we're thinking the second day will start very early, maybe two to three hours before sunup. Moonless night. And not all interstates, some small roads, go through small towns. We want this to be a tough test."

"Tell me more about security, what you're planning."

"We thought about and discarded the idea of armed guards. Just . . . no. So we'll have a following vehicle with probably two people, the passenger ready to call the cops the moment anything pops, also in radio contact with the driver and home base. We're also going to notify the state highway patrols, and all the local police and sheriffs of the locations she'll pass through, ask them to just cruise by, that's all, just be a presence now and then. If they say there are extra costs of course we'll pay those, not a problem."

"Do you anticipate trouble?"

"I'm assuming somewhere somehow there will be a leak. We've already had someone photographing our truck while out for an early test run, that's how that story got into our local newspaper. Earlier than I would have liked, but . . . I mean, I have to face the obvious. The moment this is announced—I wouldn't expect your office to do anything in secret, wouldn't ask for that—it will be front-page news. Explode. Sunday morning talk shows will be a riot. So sure, there will be a reaction. Of course there's the possibility of actual violence, but other tricks, interventions that could be done that wouldn't get people arrested."

"Such as . . . ?

The waiter returned to take away their oyster plates, asking if they were ready to order. Frank asked what Stewart was having; when he replied a blackened salmon Caesar salad Frank ordered the same.

"Here's one. Every truck that passes us—that's easy to do, we hold at the speed limit, slower if weather or traffic requires but never faster— every truck pulls in front legally, but then slows down, maybe taps the brakes, that kind of thing. Not a problem for the software, but a pain in the ass for the driver. Or simply drive by holding the horn open for the entire pass. Finger in the air, no doubt."

"Violence?

"I'll tell you the one that scares the hell out of me. Snipers. Someone on a hilltop a long way from the road."

"Man I wish I could say that won't happen, but it could. What in the world can you do about that?"

"Actually we planned on this when setting up our budget. We're going to have helicopters flying over any high land, any vantage points, keeping ahead of the truck, communicating with the cops if they see anything, also telling the truck to stop if it looks like the real thing."

"This won't go easy, will it?"

"I'm sure you know Simon Drake."

"The LCTU? Of course, met with him several times."

"Your phone will ring five seconds after the national approval news goes public, and it won't be Simon offering you best wishes. He'll be hot. He's one of the main reasons we're planning on dealing with a law that says there has to be a driver—the man is connected to Congress, has lots of loyal folks all over the country. Not just drivers, but police, food workers, construction . . . the airlines! They could cre-ate a lot of havoc."

"And your answer . . . "

"This is going to happen. If there is a law requiring a driver . . . I'll tell you what we call them in the shop, a babysitter. Not nice, I know, but if the law says there has to be a human in the cab then, well, a babysitter. Not something I'll ever say publicly. Anyway, if that happens we'll work with all concerned to create a living wage for drivers, maybe even salaries so they don't have to push the miles, but it will be a lower wage, they'll have to accept it." He leaned forward. "This change is going to happen. It is inevitable, because the technology is here, almost finished, and because shippers want to save costs, save money, whenever possible."

The waiter appeared just then with their salads. Both men having declined beverages he returned, topped off their water glasses and left.

Frank continued. "As we see it, the most logical outcome is a gradual reduction in the number of cabs with drivers in them. Wait, let me split that into two groups—actual drivers, no technology, and babysitters. Both groups gradually going away. I can't predict the timeline, but twenty years from now there won't be any humans doing long-haul driving. None, because they just aren't necessary. The technology will just keep improving and improving, just as your home computer and your television and, for sure, your cell phone have, and keep on doing so, keep on updating, able to do more better faster. Truck systems downloading software updates just like your phone does."

Stewart ate for a while, Frank held off adding more information; there was already plenty for Stewart to think about. Then Stewart said "So tell me about your driver. Why a woman, trying to make a point?"

"No, not at all. We needed someone with a clean driving record, good experience, but not in a strong financial situation and no at-home commitments. The search firm found us an excellent candidate, she just happens to be a woman. All on the up and up. We learned on our own . . . let me not compromise you with any details. I'll just say that we knew before the interview that she was what we wanted regarding finances and her family situation. In the interview she was tough, intelligent, wanting money big time, wanting to improve her situation. In other words, perfect."

In late May James Dorfmann received a letter, a standard business envelope with no return address. Inside was a note looking like it came from a standard office printer.

**Concept approved by admin. and will monitor.
System developed by MHR Bakersfield.
No date yet, but not long.**

James sat down, read the short note over several times, savoring it. He knew what he had; a possible ticket to the big time. Recognition, maybe national recognition, of his skills as an investigative reporter. At the very least he hoped this would land him a full-time position with the *Bakersfield True Post*, a paper he had read and admired since he first learned to read. He had fond memories of sitting with his father and mother as they read the paper to him, usually the funnies but occasionally a happy story about a new playground or a positive children's movie or child-friendly restaurant. As he grew they would have him pick out words he knew, so much of his English education and his enjoyment of good writing came from that exposure.

James knew he had to get this exactly right. He had promised Timmerlee some positive press, make him look good for the inevitable senatorial campaign. But the article had to be about the truck and its potential impact on truckers; people want to read about human interest first, economic impact second, bureaucrats last. He also felt time pressure; what if someone else, someone in D.C. got wind of the story, broke it first. He sat down and started to write, finding that the words came easily—he realized he'd been writing the story in his head for some time in anticipation of this moment. He didn't have much to work with, so made some reasonable guesses, knowing as he did so that if he's totally wrong it was all over for him as a reporter, wedding photos the rest of his life. But there was to be a test, and that was confirmation enough, emboldening him to make up a neutral, reasonable quote. After all, was Timmerlee ever going to say, "I never said that?" Not hardly, if James kept it neutral. He finished, edited, cut words and tightened the delivery, and at one a.m. sent it to his friend Jakub at the *Post*.

✳✳✳

EXPERIMENTAL TRUCK TO BE TESTED

The True Post has learned that a test will be held shortly of a truck that has potential to change forever the long-haul trucking industry. Based on technology that has existed for more than a decade, and advanced by Bakersfield-based MHR Investments, the truck will be steered, stopped and started by electronics that will issue commands to be carried out by systems built into the tractor, the industry name for the front end of an eighteen-wheeler. It is believed that there will be a driver behind the wheel, but that driver will take control only in the event of an emergency or system failure.

Stewart W. Timmerlee, Administrator of the National Highway Traffic Safety Administration, will have responsibility for coordinating the test with various state authorities. Although the exact route has not been disclosed, it is believed to be from somewhere in Southern California on various types of roads. Mr. Timmerlee would not confirm that the test would take place or even that the truck existed, but through a spokesman stated that his administration takes highway safety very seriously, listed statistics about

reduced truck accidents under his administration, and said that the emphasis on continuing to
reduce those, and all accidents, will continue.

James R. Dorfmann
Stringer for the *Bakersfield True Post*

Ellen took the truck out several times, all day runs, none longer than four hours. After each run she was debriefed, and the electronics were thoroughly checked. The engineers and electrical and software experts found nothing on the last two runs, so a much longer run, including night driving, was planned.

At nine in the morning the truck rolled out of Bakersfield, away from the warehouse that housed the computers and engineers' desks and the wiring equipment that allowed the truck to travel without human control, headed for Arizona.

At three-thirty the next morning the warehouse was attacked. Several sticks of dynamite, fuse lit, were flung from a passing car that kept going; the blast damaged the brick wall and destroyed cable feeds connecting the building to a nearby pole, damaging the pole, but because the explosives were not hard against the building the wall wasn't breached.

Frank was awakened by his cell phone. The adrenalin rush, the worry, resulted in instant alertness.

"Yes."

It was Walt. "Explosion outside the lab. Bomb, not doubt. No major damage, although the cables are blown to hell. Alarms triggered several blocks around, lots of cops. No one around, no one hurt."

"Shit. OK, do we have to worry about GeeCee?"

"Or the driver. Snipers?"

"Wow. Sorry. Yes, yes of course the driver."

"Keep going or stop?"

"Call you back in ten. Thanks for agreeing to be the prime contact, by the way . . . must have been fun hearing from the law at this hour."

"Not much. Conversation started 'This is Sergeant' . . . somebody, name gone already. Anyway, calls starting that way get your attention."

"Ten. Bye."

Frank peed, washed his face, decided, called.

Walt answered immediately "Less than ten. Decision is . . . "

"We know where Ellen is staying, right? Truck supposed to roll out . . . mountain time, got to get it . . . Damn, I'm sleepy and wide-awake at the same time. Can't think. OK, mountain time, gain an hour, almost five there. Supposed to go again at eight, that's seven here. So Ellen gets up around six, that's five here. OK, that's it; I'll call at five. Ellen's choice, for sure. Danger, but maybe none. Can't let the bad guys win. I mean, what the fuck, going to stop this because . . . no. Not stop."

Frank reset his alarm for five, and thinking there was nothing to be done now fell quickly asleep, but not deeply, suffering drifting, weird dreams.

At the same time the bomb was tossed in Sacramento a group of four men surprised the sole guard posted at GeeCee, moving quickly, rehearsed. The guard had only pepper spray, and couldn't get it out of the holster before the men were on him, knocking him down and wrapping his body and mouth in wide tape with their gloved hands, baseball caps pulled low over their faces. The attack took place on the far side of the truck, away from the cameras mounted on the motel. After controlling the guard they each used spray paint for one minute, then ran to their car and were quickly gone. The security tapes would be useless, no faces, backs of bodies, no license plate visible.

About half an hour after the attack a driver walked to his truck, getting an early start for the final leg of his trip, going home. He stopped when he saw the guard on the ground, as he tore the tape off the man's mouth and freed his arms he saw the spray painting, the words. He ran back to the motel, pounded the bell when there was no one at the desk. When the clerk appeared he said, "Vandalism, Walt's forwarding.

Guard on the ground. Call the cops, tell the driver." Not wanting the trouble or to lose the time, the driver quickly turned and left. The clerk checked the by-truck registration and found the name and room number of the driver. It rang a few times, then an alert voice. "Hello?"

"Miss Michel?" He pronounced it Michael. "This is the desk clerk. You're driving Walt's Forwarding, right?"

"Yes"

"We've had a report that your guard was knocked down and your truck has been vandalized. I'm very sorry. We'll call the police, check the security tapes."

She threw on clothes and rushed to the truck, the highway patrol already there, talking to the guard.

The words were sprayed on the tractor and trailer

BITCH
WHORE
SCAB
YOU NEXT TIME

Spikes had been driven into several of the wheels. The lower set of front electronics, mounted just above the bumper, was covered in spray paint.

Ellen had her phone in her hand and started to make a call. As she did so she was approached by one of the troopers. Before he could talk she told him "This is my truck. I'm the driver, Ellen Michel. Let me call the office and then I'm all yours." He nodded and stepped away.

For the second time that early morning Frank's phone sang its song. It took a moment, up from sleep; then the memory of the earlier call rushed back. Expecting an update, he was surprised to hear Ellen's voice. "Frank the truck was trashed. Guard jumped, spray paint, spikes in wheels. Gotta tow it."

"You OK?"

"Sure, I was asleep. Motel. Glad not a sleeper cab or they might have jumped me too. Highway patrol here, gotta talk to them."

"What did they spray?"

"Words of love. Scab, bitch, whore."

"I'm sorry. Really sorry. We'll get someone out to do the tow . . . You're where the itinerary said you'd be, right?"

"Right. Tell them to bring spray paint, cover the words, what do you think?"

"Of course. Good thinking."

"And replacement tires, these aren't rolling. One more, guess I should tell you everything. They also wrote that next time it would be me."

A pause. "Let me talk to one of the officers."

She turned, held out the cell to the nearest trooper. "My boss."

"Trooper Banks here."

"Trooper Banks, this is Frank Stevenson. I run the firm that's . . . that owns this truck. The driver works for us, our company. I understand one of the items sprayed is threatening to her."

"Yes sir."

"Could you please do this? Let her check out, take her to a car rental, then stay with her for a few miles, just see no one is following. We'd so appreciate that."

"Yes sir, we've got to stay here a while, we're interviewing the guard right now, have to talk to your driver—well, guess we could do that on the way to a car—and take some pictures. But yes, we can do that. Let me ask you, anyone threaten you, your company, your driver? Anyone you suspect could have done this?"

Frank paused, considering. "This is an experimental truck. You'll notice the electronics attached to the trailer and cab."

"Yes, I see them. Oh, is this the truck where the driver doesn't do the driving, the . . . equipment does? We've all been briefed on it, in fact some of our cars are going to watch for it, make a point of passing it, watch for weirdness. Sorry I didn't pick up on that."

"Trooper Banks, I think you were looking at the vandalism and the guard and talking to my driver. It certainly wasn't first on your mind, not at this hour." He sighed, took a deep breath. "You should also know that our development lab in Bakersfield was bombed last night, maybe around the same time. Sure could be a link. You might want to check in with the local police."

"Yes sir, we'll do that. Glad you told me, we'll make sure your driver is well on her way. And of course we're going to have to notify the FBI, this is interstate commerce, plus incidents in two states may be related."

"I understand. Thank you, I, we, really appreciate that. Please let me talk to my driver again, just a moment. Oh, I should ask, how is the guard?"

"Some skin hurting from where tape was used, ripped off, and he got pushed around and knocked down, but we think it is just bad bruises. Rescue's here, they're checking his vitals, treating the skin, but he's talking to us fine, don't think he's going to the hospital."

"Thanks again."

The highway patrolman gave the phone back to Ellen. "I know they're waiting to talk to you, but you should know this. Someone tried to bomb our lab, probably about the same time as the attack. Might be the same folks. No big damage, cables wrecked but the wall held."

"Shit. Scary."

"Well said. Call again when you're getting the car."

"Yep."

"Seems there should have been two guards, maybe three when GeeCee is parked for food or sleep. Big, bad error."

"Yep." She hung up.

The patrolman came back to her. "So this is that test truck, right? The one where the driver doesn't actually drive? Uh . . . sorry, no insult intended."

"That's fine, I don't drive. I can take over any time, blink of eye, but so far I haven't had to. Yes, this is that truck."

They talked a bit longer, the guard was cleared by the medics and said he was going home, aspirin and a hot bath and a shot of rye whisky. The tow truck arrived, the driver prepared for the unusual assignment of applying spray paint to the trailer before changing some tires then towing tractor and trailer away, headed for Bakersfield. Ellen quickly packed, taking time only to use the toilet and brush her hair and teeth, then got in the waiting patrol car. She realized she was very hungry but would wait until she got her rental car. The patrol car followed her for fifteen miles, dropping way back, speeding up and passing, then falling behind again. Seeing no indication she was being followed the troupers turned around. Ellen took the next exit, starved and nervous, ate a big breakfast sitting with her back to the wall. Nothing happened; she returned without incident.

Six a.m. Pacific. James Dorfmann's phone ringing. He resented the sound for just a moment, then like Frank, was instantly awake, the truck, its proposed near-future test popping into his consciousness. "Dorfmann."

"So if you're going to be the man on the scene with this truck business you need to get your lazy ass out of bed and cover the story. Or are you no longer interested?"

"Fuck off and tell me what's up."

"Not you, obviously."

"Jakub, here's the deal. Feed me good info and I'll buy you lunch today. Continue to be a jerk and I'll spread bad rumors about your sex life."

"Anything for a free feed. OK, big boy, here it is. Past three this morning someone tried to bomb the warehouse, the truck's home. Messed up the brick wall, blew an electrical pole and some cables all to hell and gone but didn't trash the warehouse, explosion a bit too far away."

"What are the police . . . "

"Oh, so you don't want to know what else happened?"

"You're a dead man."

"Ignored. The truck was attacked overnight, maybe about the same time as the pop here. Guard roughed up but mostly OK, driver was asleep in a motel bed, out of harm's way. They messed up the truck, don't have full details but spray paint was part of it. Early info is they have no info, that is, cops don't, the bad guys were careful. Trying to learn more. Here's the deal; I'm too busy with my day job to honcho this. Want to come on down and sit at an empty desk and crank up an article or two? Min usual stringer pay, maybe we can work out something more."

"On my way. Should I say thank you?"

"You should, and bring lots of money for a big lunch."

"Asshole. Thank you."

✳✳✳

EXPERIMENTAL TRUCK ATTACKED, LOCAL EXPLOSION MAY BE LINKED

The experimental truck technology reported in several recent Post articles has attracted not only curiosity but also violence, apparently from those who oppose the use of the new system.

At about three this morning an explosion, possibly dynamite, was set off near the warehouse where the truck is housed and outfitted with the electronics that will allow the truck to drive on major highways and interstates with little or no driver's guidance. The manufactures, MHR Investors, believe the system will reduce accidents and improve fuel mileage, with additional savings coming from lower wages—possibly salaries rather than per-miles or hourly payments, and in some situations without a driver behind the wheel. It is likely that concerns about losing jobs to technology sparked this incident.

About the same time as the attack in Bakersfield, the test truck was parked in a lot at a truck stop several hundred miles from here. (The authorities have asked us not to give the exact location while the investigation continues.) While the driver slept in a safe location, a guard was subdued by three or four men, the truck was spray-painted and damage was done to the tractor and trailer. Since the two incidents in two states may be connected it is believed the FBI is working with local authorities in both locations, although that has not yet been confirmed.

James R. Dorfmann

James did not add 'Stringer' after his name, and for whatever reason, it was not challenged. He didn't comment on it, but felt it portended well for future, full-time employment.

Simon Drake received a call he had rather been expecting, a request from the FBI for an interview. The meeting was set for the next day.

Morris Laymer, FBI Agent, arrived ten minutes early and was promptly shown into Simon's office. After a handshake and Morris showing his identification and badge in the large leather wallet they got right to it.

"Mr. Laymer, I'm guessing you'd like to know what the LCTU had to do with the bombing in LA and the attack on the parked truck, the experimental one. I can save you a lot of time. The answer is nothing. Is there anything else I can do for you?"

"Mr. Drake, we are not accusing anyone, and your union is not under suspicion."

"At this time."

"Mr. Drake, I'm not looking for an adversarial conversation. Please, let me finish."

Simon gave an open palmed, sweeping gesture indicating his visitor should proceed.

"It is possible that someone in your position, or one of your staff, might hear something. In addition, we'd deeply appreciate your issuing a letter—perhaps email—to everyone you can reach asking if they've heard something. The perpetrators *might* be a union member, but it could be a driver who is not in LCTU, or a family member acting independently, or just someone who hates technology, someone who thinks the government is putting people out of work by allowing this technology . . . "

"As I understand it, the attacks happened far apart at about the same time."

"Yes, that's true. But it still could be family members, could be an underground anti-technology group, sure could be an anti-government group—we've got a boatload of those. Scary folks in some of those groups. So . . . would you please consider a broadcast message, request for information?"

"We'll do it. The LCTU is made up of hard-working, loyal Americans. If they can help the FBI catch those turds they'll do so, they'll share. Do they contact you through me or you directly?"

"Here's my card. Please have them contact me." A pause. "The FBI appreciates this, Mr. Simon."

"You're welcome."

As he left, the agent thought "I'll be astounded if I get one contact." Simon Drake thought "What a bald-faced lie. Hell yes they suspect us."

James Dorfmann knew he wanted a follow-up article with the technology developers. He did his research, found out all he could about the company and Frank Stevenson. Then he called MHR, left a message that he was a reporter for the *Bakersfield True Post*, would like to interview Mr. Stevenson. He waited two days, receiving no return call he left the same message again, politely and calmly. Another two days of quiet, then as he was wondering if he should call again or write or just give up, his phone rang.

"Mr. Dorfmann, I'm calling on behalf of Frank Stevenson. He would be willing to meet with you tomorrow morning at our investment office, nine o'clock. Is that acceptable?"

"Yes, thank you so much. I'll be there." He was disappointed, hoping that the interview would take place at the warehouse; he would have liked a tour, maybe sit behind the wheel of that special truck. But he was getting his interview; as far as he knew the first reporter to do so.

James had made a decision about how he would open the interview, and did so. "Thank you, sir, for this interview. I wanted to make sure you knew I was the reporter… perhaps I should say photographer who took those first pictures of your truck."

"I, we, know that. Good work on your part. As I said to our staff, it could happen at any time, although a bit more opportunity for research before going public would have been preferred. Not important now . . . so, where would you like to start?"

"Your company, MHR, helps people and corporations grow wealth through investments. MHR has never been known as a venture capital firm, yet this is exactly what you've done with the driverless technology; you've backed a high-tech development that might fail or might have tremendous upside potential, traditional venture capital structure. How, or why, the branching out?"

"That's the second time I've been asked that. Not yet, but some day I'll tell you who asked. The answer . . . an article appeared in a business magazine about our company, our success rate, and in the interview I said something about the bright future of American technology. That comment was read by Walt Wizniski. Walt was working for an auto parts manufacturer, but he was certain that the development of self-driving vehicles, especially trucks, was moving far too slowly. He came to us with his concept, plus some patents he'd developed. Fortunately we had some cash on hand that wasn't doing much, interest rates down and the market healthy but flat. I certainly got some cautionary comments from my best people, but I own the company and took the plunge. We developed a separate arm, brought Walt on board as chief engineer, got going. Hired some great technical people, software engineers, designers. Look James, there is no doubt that if our technology, T O T, gets federal approval we are going to make back our investment several times over. At some point we'll likely sell it all to Walt and others, leveraged buyout, we'll take our money and, who knows, get into something else futuristic, or maybe just go back to stocks and bonds and occasionally brilliantly shorting the market."

"You have a female test driver. Was the choice of a woman deliberate?"

"Also asked that before, same person. I really owe you the name, I promise, maybe right after the national test. Answer; not at all, not one bit. We were looking for an experienced driver who fit our specifications, and it turned out to be a woman."

"Those specifications being . . . "

"I'd rather not say. Just a good, appropriate background. I will tell you that she was independent, so it was easier to recruit her than a company driver."

"If approved and successful, and my guess both will happen, there are lots of drivers who will be out of work. Do you, your company, have any comment on that?"

Frank paused a long pause; James waited. "We don't see things happening right away, jobs dropping off a cliff . . . perhaps ten years or more. But yes, eventually it could be a million truck-driving jobs gone. My hope is that several things happen over those many years. The first is retraining in some other skill, perhaps high-tech manufacturing and assembly. More of those jobs are being brought back from overseas, computer chips being a prime example. The second is up to Congress, but I'm assuming there will be something such as an early social security entry exemption, a special retirement fund, something. And, as I said, retraining, but funded by state or federal governments, not the individual."

"One more, and thank you again for this interview. Perhaps some day you'll let me tour the development facility, maybe . . . sit behind the wheel? Engine off, of course."

"Sure. Not yet, but I'll make that happen eventually. Is that your question?"

"No, sorry, daydream just slipped out." Frank chuckled. "Mr. Stevenson, what have you learned that you didn't know when this started?"

A brief, considering pause by Frank. "Two things. Of course a whole lot about trucks, trucking companies, shipping and receiving, applicable regulations and laws . . . a lot. But also how brilliant engineers and software designers and computer folks and metal fabricators can design and install all the parts so a truck can steer by computer instruction, not by a human. Dazzling, brilliant people all. I get caught up in what we're doing, dealing with so many issues and problems, trying to get to an end goal, I rarely think about it, about them. But once in a while it hits me, I stop and say 'Wow'. . . . These are talented, splendid individuals."

CHAPTER ELEVEN

Frank Stevenson received a letter asking for a meeting, signed by Paul and Henry Reed. His secretary called the number included in the letter and set it up. When they arrived it was explained to them that they would have to be patted down. Paul and Henry were surprised but accepted, after which they were introduced to Frank. They were both dressed in suits; Henry carried a small leather briefcase, which also had been inspected.

The office was comfortable but not ornate. A plain wooden desk with a computer, two visitor armchairs, some pictures of birds and landscapes, a couch and three more armchairs around a low table. On the table and the desk were landline phones; Frank had used only a cell phone until the past several weeks, when concerns about spying had increased for Frank and his staff, all of whom now had landlines. As happened this time, visitors, except for those well known, were patted down, briefcases checked.

Frank was standing as they entered, shook hands with both. "Hello, glad to meet you. Please be seated." He indicated the couch. "Which one is Paul, which Henry?"

"I'm Paul."

"Making me Henry."

"Good. Sorry about the pat down, but with all that's happened I'm sure you understand. You'll notice my windows are all covered with drapes, can't see the beautiful view. Chose this location in part 'cause of great views from most of the offices, now drapes and artificial lights. Sucks, it does. I've told my staff that if anyone wants to leave they can,

I'll give them a good recommendation, not blame them for leaving. Had one guy take me up on it, about to be a father for the first time, sure understand. Everyone else hanging in there, bless their hearts."

The Reed brothers nodded their heads.

"So enough complaining. What's on your minds, how can I help you?"

Henry spoke first. "Paul and I are one year apart. I'm older. After my first year in college . . . wait, I have to tell you our father was a truck driver, long hauls. He's off the road now, works in a hardware store and builds furniture, tables and chairs mostly, sells them. Happy guy, and Mom's glad he's home now. Gone all the time the first thirty years of their marriage. Anyway, he's well set . . . they're well set, she—Mom—went to college, he didn't, she's taught kindergarten for a long time. House paid for, money in the bank. So back to the story. Dad was an independent trucker, and we both rode with dad on some of his shorter trips. Loved it, not boring . . . "

Paul took up the conversation. "So dad comes to us with an idea during my senior year, Henry in college. He says he'll front the money for us to rent or lease an eighteen-wheeler. I'm turning 18 middle of the year, so dad's plan is I go into truck driver's school right away after graduation, Henry does too, same class, we get our licenses and then jump in dad's leased truck and drive till we drop. Well, not drop. Bad choice of words."

Henry again. "The rules are we have to pass a test, get our CDLs, but don't have to go to a truck driver's school, don't need a certificate. Well, we've got a great school, our dad. He takes us out as often as he can; we drive in all kinds of conditions. It was an easy learn for both of us, I think because we had ridden with him in past years, kind of in our blood. This is near the end of his being on the road; he wanted to get us going and then retire from driving.

Paul continued. "We got one with a sleeper, and just drove loads as independent contractors all over California. Pick up a load at the docks in San Diego, head north to warehouses, pick up a load from some factory in Anaheim or Vista headed for the Oakland docks or back to San Diego. Highway hours, grinding. Top to bottom in our fair state is twelve to fourteen hours, depending on destination, so one drives, one sleeps. Stop to eat, take a shower and change clothes, some ten-minute walks in a picnic area at a rest stop just so we can see grass and lean against a tree. Sometimes when we can't stand it we use a motel, eat a really good meal and sleep in a real bed, but not often. Not often. Drive, pile up the miles and dollars. Short summer that first one, but every summer after that from the moment school was out until it started we drove. Did paperwork, invoices, in booths at diners or those motel rooms. Learned how to do it, learned how to run our two-person rolling business. Missed a lot of parties, beer, sex . . . "

"We like to think so. . . . "

"But we knew we'd have a hell of a good next egg after graduation. We paid for the truck, that is, paid dad back for the lease the first year, so the truck was all on us, every summer after the first we had the money in the bank to start a new lease, down payment. Mom and dad paid for college, most of it, so we could come out of college with a hunk of money each, enough to get going in life. I got a degree in business, Paul liberal arts but took several accounting courses . . . "

"Dad said, and Henry too, that it would be a good thing if I could understand a basic spreadsheet, profit and loss . . . "

Frank interrupted. "Excuse me, I'm being a lousy host. Either of you want something to drink—coffee, water, juice . . . ?"

"Juice, thanks. Any kind" said Paul. Henry nodded. "Same, thank you."

"OK, I'll be healthy too." Frank rose, went to the office door, opened it and spoke briefly, then returned, leaving the door slightly open, and returned to his seat. "Please continue."

Paul took up the thread. "I'm thinking we're giving you too much background, taking too much time. Here's why we asked to see you. We own a small trucking firm, local and medium runs, almost all under a hundred miles. But we've wanted to get into the long haul business from the start, in our blood. We know the business, drove thousands of miles, both of us."

Orange and apple juice appeared on a tray, glasses with ice. The clerk closed the door on his way out.

Henry leaned forward. "We want to equip our fleet with your system, all six trucks. It means letting go the six drivers we have now, over time, and that won't be easy. Not saying we're like a family, but we do know them well, some of their spouses and kids. Paul and I are working with our accountant to see how much of a severance we can offer. Even a small something for the part-time, fill-in drivers we occasionally use. Good recommendations, good severance, but still won't be a pleasant time."

"But good drivers can find work fairly easily, right? Trucking firms looking for drivers."

"Yes, but we almost never have overnight runs, and we offer good benefits, and the personal touch of a brothers-owned company, brothers who have been truckers. No union, no union dues, we're too small for the LCTU to bother with. Oh, they've poked at us a few times, but our drivers took a pass."

Paul spoke. "Henry and I have crunched and crunched the numbers. Deal is we see a payback, come out ahead in four to six years per vehicle with no driver. Gets really good after that. Your system costs one hundred thousand, right?"

"We're going to bring the price down. One hundred now, but like anything there are savings as the technology improves, keep up quality and increase quantity. Six? We could deal. I want them out there, being used, getting publicity. If you two . . . what's your firm's name?"

The brothers answered as one. "Brothers Quality Delivery."

"If you two . . . do you call it BQD . . . ?

They nodded.

"If BQD starts using the system, offering to deliver goods for some percent below what the major haulers charge . . . "

"At least ten percent" said Paul. "At least. We might be able to offer twenty percent lower. Blow the competition out of the water, you can see that."

Frank poured his juice; the brothers took a moment to do the same. Frank took a drink and held his glass, turning it in his hands. "Yes, and my phone would ring. Good for us all, looks like." He paused, turning his glass, looking at it, then up at his visitors. "You're both wearing wedding rings. Children?"

Paul answered. "Beat my big brother. I've got one, he doesn't yet but his wife says 'they're trying.' I've offered to give Henry some advice, explain things to him but he tells me he's good to go, understands it. I hope so."

Frank smiled, then it faded. "At some point, some time in the future, driverless trucks will be as normal as cell phones. The industry will change, no doubt about it. There is no way to hold back technology, no way to stop something happening if it helps industry do things faster or cheaper or better or safer or . . . but that isn't today, not this year or certainly not the next several years. This system puts drivers out of work. Flat does, can't hide that. It also allows for drivers to sit in the trucks and do nothing, if that is what the law requires, but I think Congress won't pass that law, way too much pushback from major corporations. Major donors, that is. Or perhaps a two-step evolution; first with drivers, then eventually without them. We'll see. Oh, by the way, we're calling the system T O T, stands for truck operation technology. I'm not crazy about it, but it seems to be sticking. But I wander . . . back to about you, your families."

Frank emptied the rest of the apple juice into his glass, drank about half, put the glass down. He sat with his hands together, leaning forward, eyes firmly on one brother then the other, back and forth.

"Someone has to be first. You two certainly look like prime candidates—you're educated, understand business concepts, better, you understand the trucking business. You've driven thousands of miles in an eighteen-wheeler. You're running a delivery firm, truck delivery. Can't think of better resumes to take this on. But you certainly know about the violence—blessing no one has been killed yet, but close, too damn close. I'll have to introduce you to our test driver, Ellen Michel.

Tough lady, I admire the hell out of her. Threatened, truck trashed, she didn't blink. I offered her an out with a decent severance several times. Finally she says, 'I got the idea—let it be. If I want out I know where to find you.' Haven't spoken about her leaving again, don't think she's leaving until our agreement ends, which is when the feds approve us, whenever that is. I don't doubt we'll get federal approval for driverless trucks, but I'm not predicting the date, not going to jinx it."

Paul looked concerned. "So approval puts her out of work."

"No, I mean that's correct, but the agreement is that she is our test driver, test pilot until the feds say T O T is legal, with or without a driver required, although if I had to bet on what Congress will do, initially a driver will be required. As I said, I think it will be phase-out, some kind of slow, steady transfer to driverless. Standing by for Congress in its wisdom to speak. Anyway, agreement is then she gets out with a generous check in her hands. At least, it seemed generous at the time, but I'm thinking we'll add some more—kind of hazardous duty pay. I won't comment on her long term plans, but I can say she'll be well fixed and far away in a place she wants to go to, don't know if the bad guys will keep looking for her. She might even use a different name, not sure. But she's cool with that, same as she is about keeping going in spite of the bomb and threats and hate mail."

Paul nodded. "I know where you're going with this family thing. Ellen will move away, she won't be the focus. The focus will be any company that actually starts using the system . . . uses T O T, so if that's us we get the trouble, not Ellen."

"That's exactly right. As I said to Ellen when we hired her, we're talking about a million drivers, many but not all LCTU, either out of work or taking a significant pay cut. I don't blame LCTU for the violence, don't really believe they planned attacks in a back room. I mean that. But there are hundreds of thousands of people who just might want to, at the very least, vandalize trucks, at the worst throw a bomb through your window. Do the math, gentlemen. If only one-half of one percent of a million drivers is willing to risk major jail time—maybe life—to strike out, that's *five thousand* potential bad guys. And bad girls. Five thousand who might take extreme action."

"We've both talked to our wives about this" answered Paul. "I've got a two year old, want him to be safe, and of course our wives. We've made arraignments for them to live elsewhere for a year or so. We'll stay here, probably live together . . . "

"And gain weight from pizza and beer . . . " Henry injected.

"Probably right about that. Anyway, here's our thinking, and I mean all four of us. Somebody is going to do this. This technology exists today, and it is going to be on trucks around the world in ten years, or twenty years. . . . don't know exactly when but there is no doubt, none, that its coming. So here's our choice as we see it. If we do it first there are potential problems, even real danger. We'll have guards at our house and office for that, and family far away for. . . . for too long. But see, if we aren't the first, or worse, if one of the giants with dozens, a hundred or more drivers makes the first move then we're too late to the dance. The first company that mounts T O T on all their trucks will have a big leg up, it's that simple. We don't think we have a choice. Really don't. Oh, and we'll keep doing short runs, in-city runs. We'll keep some of our drivers for that, maybe all if we can expand that part of our business. We'd like to not lay off any of our drivers, and if the rollout of T O T goes well and we can keep, maybe increase, our other delivery business we quite possibly can do just that. Over time some may retire or go to other firms or, who knows, other kinds of jobs, so if all works out well we never lay off anyone. As I said, that's our goal."

Henry nodded. "We're going to do everything we can to help build a strong team, keep the drivers we need by adding more short routes, small package deliveries, maybe food or medicine; we're looking at lots of options. Not that the team isn't already strong; we have a good, strong relationship with our employees, loyalty both ways, both directions. But we see that we're going to have some costs in addition to the T O T equipment—maybe pay raises, and for sure guards, alarm systems—but we can absorb costs now in return for this opportunity."

"That's how we see it" Paul added. "The phrase once-in-a-lifetime is overused, but it absolutely applies here. One chance in a lifetime for BQD to be a leader—*the* leader—in the trucking industry."

Henry reached in his briefcase, took out a manila envelope and extracted several sheets of charts, estimated profit and loss projections, estimated corporate growth, occasionally pointing to them as he spoke. "As we've said, we have good, reliable drivers, pay them well. Neither of us want turnover, want to be spending any more time recruiting than we have to. Right now that time is zero."

Paul nodded agreement.

"Because we have lots of short and medium runs we pay some work by the hour, long haul of course by the mile. If the law requires us to have a driver sitting there watching, for at least several years until we can go driverless . . . for those drivers who take on the those assignments, the T O T trucks, we're going to switch to salaries, first salaried interstate drivers I've heard of. That way they know they're getting a steady paycheck, whatever their driving responsibilities. However, it will be on the lower end of their average annual earnings. Quite simply, they will not make as much as before; it won't be punishing, but it will be less. They can take it or leave it. We'll certainly say it more graciously than that, but that's the message. Get paid a flat salary, some reduced from your best years but still decent, sit and watch the truck or leave. Again, if the law makes us."

"Here's an advantage of salaries you may not have considered" Frank added. "The Truck Operation Technology is structured to go exactly the speed limit, no more. Of course it goes slower, T O T slows down depending on traffic and weather, but pay by the mile doesn't work well for drivers that can't exceed the speed limit, even a little . . . three miles over the limit makes a real difference when your haul is New York to Minneapolis or Houston or San Diego. You, your employees won't have that problem."

"That's true" Paul agreed. "What is also true is that I'm a coffee addict. I'm sorry, is there any coffee available? Just plain black is fine.

My brother is too gracious to ask for it, but he'd also use a cup. Helps him think. But he adds milk or some such. I don't understand, but . . . "

Frank laughed. "Sure, I don't drink it, don't think of it, sorry . . . but my wife does, I should have asked. The staff says the coffee is acceptable . . . that's what they call it, 'acceptable.'" He stood and walked to the office door, opened it and made a request as before. The coffee appeared soon, with a small pitcher of milk and a selection of sweeteners.

Henry shuffled his papers, pulled out a sheet, put it on top. "OK Frank, all that was the windup, here's the pitch. We will put T O T on all six eighteen wheelers as quickly as possible, offer shipping discounts, see how much business we can pull in how fast. We'll have guard vehicles following them for a few trips, don't know yet how many."

Frank interjected "If you're the only firm with T O T you'll be the target—sorry, not a pretty word—but you'll be the target of the bad guys. But if several companies sign up right after you do, if there are a few hundred equipped trucks out there, then the heat is off you, or at least spread around."

"That's true," said Henry "so publicity works for us and against us—puts the heat on us but could also bring several others on board, maybe quickly. As you said, spread the heat around. So . . . " He turned the top document around so Frank could read it as he spoke.

"We've got a great balance sheet, strong credit. We'd like to ask you, your firm, to carry the paper for the first two setups, with a short payback. After that we can go to our bank and say 'See, this works, we want to rig more of our trucks,' We're thinking we can add one a year, maybe faster. Depends on business of course, but at most five years, our other four trucks, in that time. We'll be incurring debt but lowering expenses, and anyway, as we said, we're afraid the big boys will T O T-up and we'll miss the parade."

"Sure, we can make that work. Yes, a good plan."

Paul said, "Wait, I'm sorry, one more question. I know the system, T O T, I know T O T can be affixed to the tractor, top, sides."

"And above the bumper, low view of the road" added Frank.

"Yes. My, our question, is about the rear camera. There is one on the back of the trailer, right?

"That's right, top back."

"But we switch trailers, everyone does. What about that back camera?"

"As you said, the T O T technology will be permanently fixed to the tractor, front and sides. The side ones are actually two cameras, one looking right down next to the cab, see if there is someone next to, or close to, it. The other is pointed backward; between the two the whole sides are covered, plus back some distance. Oh, and a forward-facing camera looking at the rear-view mirrors. The hitch is the rear camera. As you said, a truck, a tractor, might pick up several trailers in a run to several locations, several states. What to do about that?"

"What did you decide?"

"At first we thought the side cameras would cover us, but someone could be in something small, even a motorcycle, and might not show up from those side shots. So we've designed an inexpensive camera that broadcasts to the cab. It has strong magnets on the bottom, stick to the metal, has a release bar. Can also have a clamp to hold it if needed."

"Sounds like a minor pain, a time waster, for someone. No driver, it would have to be the folks at the terminal."

"Exactly right. Initially someone at the terminal would have to move the camera from the inbound trailer to the outbound. Not doubt some will get lost, broken . . . terminals will have to keep several on hand, locked up of course. The goal is someday to have all trailers, tankers, flatbeds, all big rigs . . . have them all built with the camera installed. Someday. Meanwhile, the cameras can be quickly synched with the computer in the truck's cab."

"But won't that require someone in the terminal to make sure they're synched? Won't the terminals be reluctant to take on that extra responsibility?" Henry asked.

Frank responded. "Throughout all this we've seen gain-a-cost lose-a-cost. Of course the lost costs far exceed the gained, thousands of dollars of net improvement, profit potential. But there are new costs, gained costs, such as extra cameras in storage at warehouses and pay-ing the terminal or shipping firm a small premium for the extra work. Here's something important; T O T will be set up so the truck won't start rolling until the rear camera is talking to the cab computer, so someone will have to be trained, although it really isn't more that pushing a button. Really simple, put the camera on the trailer, make sure the magnets have a firm hold, turn on the computer and wait for them to synch, connect. Anyone who can operate a cell phone or a TV remote will be able to handle it. Will the trucking firm have to reimburse the shipper for extra labor time, extra expense? Sure. But the trucking firm will be ahead by a whole lot of money. Drivers cost a whole lot of money, and there won't be any."

CHAPTER TWELVE

Frank Stevenson was comfortable dealing with high-level government administrators, millionaire and billionaire investors, politicians, but was slightly nervous about his upcoming meeting with federal highway administrator Stewart Timmerlee, and so prepared carefully. Although the meeting wasn't until one thirty, he flew into Washington a day early so as to be rested, freshly shaved and showered and wearing a serious dark blue suit, white shirt, modest tie when making his pitch.

Frieda Shippens escorted Frank into Stewart's office, where the two greeted each other, then Frank indicated they should sit in the comfortable chairs near a couch, away from Frank's desk. A sign of respect.

"Mr. Timmerlee . . . "

"Stewart, please, and may I call you Frank? I try to stay informal unless the situation demands it."

"My pleasure, thank you. I, we, have a request. I saw your comment on the technology that could lead to driverless trucks. I'm assuming you know that MHR, my company, is backing the development of that technology for an eighteen-wheeler.

"Yes, that's right."

Things are going very well, we've had a few short runs, but we want to take it out for a national test, let the press know, full coverage. We will have a driver behind the wheel, but that driver will not touch the steering wheel, nor the pedals or shift lever. The driver, the human, will sit there doing nothing. There will be cameras on the driver's hands and feet, broadcasting to a limited number of sites. We can discuss that.

If all goes as we expect that recording would then be shared with the world, nightly news, maybe the same day.

"And you want this department's, what, blessing? Support?"

"There will be national coverage, which means traffic will be interrupted as everyone wants to get a look. Support from highway patrol, make that patrols, for sure, plus maybe some sheriffs or others . . . so blessing, support, yes. We want, sorry, we're asking for your office to help us set it up, eliminate barriers, maybe sanction is a good word. Sanction. We certainly aren't asking for an endorsement, just approval for us to go rolling on interstates and state highways."

"You're right about the patrols, and maybe others. That translates into overtime, those sheriffs and patrol commanders won't appreciate that, not at all."

"Anticipated, and reimbursement already in our budget. We want to be as small a pain for everyone as possible."

"Where, what route are you considering?"

"Our place in Bakersfield California, converted warehouse where we store the truck—GeeCee we call her—and do the research."

"You got bombed there, right, and your truck attacked. Driver all right? And GeeCee? Sorry, I'm asking multiples, should let you answer."

"Glad to answer. Route is Bakersfield north, not sure how far. Have to talk to mayors and highway patrol and a lot of other folks. Not just steaming down smooth interstates, no, much more. We want to go through small towns, two-lane roads for sure, sharp turns, and some kind of nighttime test, maybe road blocked in the middle of the night. We'll find some place where a state route, two lane road, crosses another similar route way out in the countryside, tight turn for sure. Maybe several of those. One or more detours. And, ahh, next . . . oh, the bombing. Didn't hurt anything inside the building, serious damage to electrical equipment outside. And the truck was damaged, vandalized, while the driver was sleeping during a road test. Driver fine, sound asleep in the motel. And GeeCee stands for game changer. Corny, yes, but that's it."

"But about the bombing, I'd like to ask you about protest against what you're doing. Legitimate protest, not violence. Do you mind if I ask you about the challenges, pushback, you are facing? I know about House Bill one one four, and I'm guessing there are others objecting."

"Absolutely. You'd be doing me a favor, helping me get ready for the press, politicians. Fire away, please."

"Let's start here in D.C. All those elected representatives up on the hill are going to want to satisfy their constituents, and those folks, those voters, middle-class middle-American voters, are going to side with the truckers. The companies will just have to go along with it. One one four seems to be just lying there, no one picking up on Representative Williams' speech. I think he made the speech to go on record, nothing wrong with that, but he's not pushing hard. Anyway, I think the middle-class voting block will keep drivers in trucks."

"I'm sorry, I don't see it that way. Of course those voters will have big objections to driverless trucks, fear of the unknown, lack of trust in the science, and what about their brother-in-law the truck driver? It will be a hard sell, but the companies and their lobbyists will bang the drum hard about saving the consumer money. You can imagine the pitch: 'These trucks will deliver goods for much less, and we'll pass those savings on to you. Groceries, televisions, furniture, everything that comes by truck will cost less because the shipping costs are lower.' Like that. Mister and missus America will say they sure are sorry about those fine truckers getting laid off, but do you know what cereal costs these days? Get it from the factory to my kitchen table for less? Yes indeed, put those cameras on those trucks."

"If the savings are indeed passed on."

Frank nodded in agreement. "Some will be, some won't. Not something I can control, that's for sure. Here's another thing. The corporations will want the science in place if it saves them money, just will. Some companies hire trucking firms, some have their own fleets. It doesn't matter. I don't believe for one minute a company is going to stand by watching while Congress is passing laws that keep their costs up. *Up?*

That makes no sense. I mean, sure, they might talk about their wonderful drivers, loyal employees, and mean every word of it. But if they can lay off most of them, hell all of them, and cut labor costs to damn near zero don't you think they'd do it? Better—the first one does it; they all do it. One company, maybe a real small one that has fifteen, twenty trucks, equips them all and then goes to the market and says I'll carry your freight for twenty percent less, forty percent less. End of story. They all do it."

"But the equipment costs money, what is it, around one hundred thousand a truck?"

"A brief detour, if I may. If a sneeze takes three seconds from beginning to clear-headed, just three seconds, do you know how far a truck goes at seventy miles per?"

"More than a hundred feet . . . two hundred?"

"Try a football field, one hundred yards . . . actually a bit into the end zone. Best driver in the world, one sneeze at the wrong time and you've got . . . well, you know what you could have. One hundred yards, blind. And, as of course you know, there are over four thousand deaths from big rig crashes a year, and if the driver is found at fault the settlement is easily a half million dollars. I'm sure a lot of those accidents are because some idiot in a sedan cut off an eighteen-wheeler, no, likely almost all of them, but that's still a lot of dead folks, settlement or not. And the list, the whole long list; worker's comp, taxes, health insurance, retirement, on and on. Gone or almost gone. So you spend one hundred K to equip a truck—I'm saying you get that back in savings damn fast, and it is all gravy from there. Simple—your competitor can cut costs in half or more, and pass those savings on to customers, and you don't do it, you are done. Outabusiness. It's that simple."

Frank paused, continued. "With rare exception, and I mean that, really rare, American truck drivers are the best. Good people, conscientious, damn hard working. They care about driving, they care about safety. Yes, damn good people. I'd stack them against drivers or workers anywhere in the world. The reality is that there is tremendous pressure on drivers, those that want to make a good living. The average in a year is about one-hundred-twenty-five thousand miles. Hard to get my head around, but what's even harder to think about is that is roughly five hundred miles a day in a five-day week. That's a haul for sure; some of it relatively easy highway miles, but certainly not all. Want to make the quota but drive fewer per day? Leave home, drive seven days a week, come home . . . some day. It just isn't easy, no way it can be easy."

Stewart Timmerlee paused, reflected on their conversation. "Don't know where I heard or read it, but there's a saying that goes 'If all the Chevys are made by robots, who will have the money to buy Chevys?' You're talking about dumping one million or more middle-class wage earners on the job market in a short period of time, many with a high school education and pretty much one skill, no longer in demand. Talk about a shock to the system!"

"Maybe not that short a period of time; most likely ten years at least. But yes, a million or more. Yes, a serious shock to the economic system. Not up to us, my company or your administration, up to Congress, but I'm guessing the answer will be financial settlements, retraining, and likely some kind of grandfathering in of present drivers."

CHAPTER THIRTEEN

Walt said, "You know, I've been thinking about T O T, and how it reads signs . . . I had an idea. Maybe a new business for us, hey?"

"I'd like to dig out of our financial hole a bit first, but lay it on me. What?"

"Frank, you know those systems that let an eligible, locked truck to go past weigh stations? The stations now talk to the laptop or phone in the cab, newest don't have to drive under those transponders on poles, pick any lane, the two computers talk to each other right now. They have like an invisible zone, drive through it and the phone and the system talk to each other, about two miles out from the weigh station. So the system just says 'keep going' or 'pull in.' Neat, huh. So that got me wondering what else T O T could chat with other computers about."

"Such as . . . "

"Accident ahead ten miles, stay in left lane. Truck stop full. Long wait for fuel. Or truck stop empty. Here's one: say you live in an apartment building with a large laundry room. There's an app that lets you know how many washers dryers available. So how about how many shower stalls open at the stop. Or put your name in; get in line for a shower. Detour warning, best to take alternate route X. Like that."

"Walt, I'd tell you you're a genius but then you might leave me and start your own company. But I think you're on to something. You want to take one of the staff, spend some hours noodling it, sure. Thanks."

CHAPTER FOURTEEN

Simon Drake had been head of the LCTU for seven years. Over that time he had, at least once a year, met with his predecessor, Karl Umbler. Karl kept up on the news, and was a great advisor and devil's advocate before Simon took a new idea to his board. They met at their favorite lunch spot, only two blocks from LCTU headquarters.

Simon asked "OK, so you've read a summary of HB one one four, read Williams's fine rant, what do you think?"

"Not only a summary, but read the bill. Not that long, pretty well written as Congressional English goes. So . . . What do *you* think?"

A waiter appeared, asked what they wanted for lunch and to drink. Both said coffee. The waiter took their orders, leaving a small basket of rolls.

Simon reached for a roll, smoothed on some of the whipped chive butter served in a cold white ramekin, bit and chewed and swallowed before answering.

"Well it is an interesting situation, political one, that's for sure. What do the various groups say? Let's look . . . " The rest of the roll was now used as a pointer at an imaginary whiteboard. "What will the truckers say? That's easy. The drivers themselves, whether or not they're LCTU members, they will say no to babysitting, to sitting in a cab watching a computer drive. Embarrassing and boring, to say the least. Plus they know, or should, that there will be a cut in pay. Big cut, probably. They'll talk about safety, loss of jobs, just like Williams said. Scare the public. Right or wrong, get people to say that they'll vote the rascals out of office if they dare to put those robots on wheels on the highways."

Simon continued. "But how about the money and influence folks? If you could take away the costs of drivers, all the recruiting and pay-roll and taxes and accidents and let them deliver tomatoes or televi-sions for half the cost, hell yes they'd want it. Every trucking firm, every company that has a fleet of trucks . . . they'd look at this totally differently. Let's say you could cut the cost of diesel fuel by half, but a lot of refinery workers would be out of work. Or tires. What if you could make tires last double the miles on eighteen-wheelers, but some, lots, of tire-making folks would be out of work. There is no doubt, none, that the trucking companies would embrace that fuel or those tires. So this is somewhat squirrely because it is drivers, hard to think of trucks without drivers, and they are humans, humans with families and mortgages and . . . all that. But savings are savings. Fifty percent cut in costs is fifty percent, and if this really comes to pass over years we're talking about a whole lot more than fifty percent from today's costs. And then everything can go down . . . those tomatoes and televisions and everything that travels by truck can be cheaper, cheaper to the American public because the trip from there to here doesn't take so many clams."

"Or no savings to the public, just bigger profits, said cynic I."

"Well, cynic, I'm thinking some company would offer a price cut on something, get a competitive edge, or at least not rise as fast as inflation. And more . . . ah, future stuff . . . but to continue . . . "

Karl nodded. "Please do."

"They won't want to say it out loud, but all the companies will want the technology, will want to eliminate the drivers. Our drivers, our members. However—big however—I'm thinking it still it will be a hell of a battle to get to that point. We've already seen some vandalism, which could get worse, lots of posturing in Congress. And the big firms will have to come up with money, talk about the options. In short, this will take time."

Simon continued. "Say the average long-hauler today makes about seventy K a year. So the new contracts say that the present driver keeps putting away seventy, but new hires, well, they sit in the trucks and go for a ride, don't do a damn thing, make thirty or thirty-five a year. Fewer accidents, *lots* fewer accidents because these machines are never sleepy or distracted because they have to take a whiz or go too fast in bad weather because they're paid by the mile or just because computers can do some things better than humans. You know, I once bought a car that had those paddles under the steering wheel; you could set the car on automatic or switch it to use the paddles, pretend you were in a Formula One at Monte Carlo or some damn thing. Tried the paddles for a week or so but figured out the computer could shift up and down a hell of a lot smoother than I could, at exactly the right RPM points. Never used the paddles again. So these truck computers will save gas. You know, automatic transmissions save wear and fuel because every shift is optimal, an easy task for a computer. But brakes will get less wear because the vehicle will always obey the speed limit, never tailgate, never have to be hard on the brakes unless some fool up ahead is, well, foolish. So as close to minimum wear as possible, and because it is never sleepy or never sneezes or never speeds it is just plain safe, safer that the world's best driver. *Safer.* So the guy, or gal, sits on his or her ass for thirty-five K a year and it is all good."

"The drivers who are grandfathered in at seventy won't say it is all good for their future brothers and sisters in the LCTU."

"But they'll take it"

"But . . . yes, I agree, they'll take it. Here's a question. . . . "

The waiter returned with their lunch orders, a BLT with a hard fried egg added for Simon, a Greek salad for Karl.

Karl continued. "It is hard to find drivers. Ads for them all the time, back of trucks saying 'come drive for us'. . . ."

"True."

"So how does cutting pay in half solve that problem? Doesn't it make it a whole lot worse?"

"Thought about that, two answers. I'm sure you remember when there was a deal cut in the auto industry, autoworkers. To keep jobs from moving out, leaving America, the agreement was that everyone on the payroll would continue at the present wage, gigantic grandfather clause. But any new hires, anyone hired one moment after the new contract was signed, came in at a little over half the former wage. Half! So answer one is that the auto companies found workers. You know, if you don't want the job then I'll take it, like that. They were able to find workers, the auto industry that is; wages going up over time and good benefits, including tuition assistance, and lots of job security. Take a lower wage, get these benefits, jobs won't leave the country.

"And second answer . . . "

Let's say the trucking industry can't find workers, drivers. Or there is violence, or threats against anyone who will take the job. Worse scenario, every trucker in America refuses to drive. Stops commerce cold. Nothing moving, just rail but that can't begin to fix it."

Karl asked, "So they win? Wages stay up, even if they're only sitting there?"

"Nope. It is one thing for Congress to vote for the working man or woman . . . . OSHA, minimum wage, workers' comp . . . something else again to vote there has to be a driver, but lower paid, and drivers strike. America shuts down. Reverse that vote so fucking fast your head spins. Nope. Either accept it, best deal you can get, thirty-five K or so a year, maybe mid-forties at best, or Congress lets driverless trucks run. Can you imagine the howling from industry and the trucking firms and the railroads that couldn't offload their piggybacks and . . . and food all over the country stops moving by truck? And cars. Cars! Shut down all those car haulers going to dealerships? Not happening. Quickest law ever passed. If they vote drivers yes— that there has to be a driver— and the drivers don't show up for their thirty-five or so and they walk out, well, Congress flips that like I said, head-spinning fast. Sit in a truck and make some money, make your reduced but still money paycheck, or sit at home and watch the trucks roll by on autopilot while you earn nada, that's their choice. Congress will go either way, but Congress won't hold on to a law, one one four, that drivers then rebel against, put commerce in the toilet. Like I said, if they pass one one four and there are no drivers showing up, the law is out the window in minutes. World record for a government changing its mind."

Karl thought about that wisdom, nodded his head. "Okay my friend, just us two LCTU leaders sitting here, private conversation. I think that's not what's going to happen, I mean, lower-wage drivers sitting in the cab watching the computer drive. Nope, I think there will be no drivers. No truckers, except short-haul. Not right away, maybe not for years, but it's coming. I'm guessing, wisdom of my years, that there will be a slow phaseout of drivers, some percent a year. Eventually, comes the day, no long-haul men and women. None. Not tomorrow, but sooner than fifty years. Maybe . . . twenty or so. The point is, mister president, if you want a strong union you're going to have to expand your base. You are going to lose tens of thousands of members. Not quickly of course, and that's way to your advantage. But replace them you'll have to do. More police forces? Maybe private security firms? And horn in on service workers, clerical folks, government employees of all kinds. Teachers? Not easy, none of them. So the bad news, Simon, is sure as the sun comes up in the morning you're going to lose a ton of members. Good news is you have time to plan and work to replace them. Time, but not a lot . . . you and your staff better get humping the moment you get back to the office."

CHAPTER FIFTEEN

Even before she drove her father's car in the empty parking lot of a closed strip mall in Detroit, just fourteen but tall for her age, Oreena Jones knew she wanted to drive, and that experience confirmed it. Her father had granted the driving wish as a birthday present, but she asked for repeated sessions, granted two or three times a month, including in heavy rain, in ice and snow. She began studying for the driver's exam shortly after turning fifteen, passing it easily as soon as old enough, then sought every opportunity to run errands for the family, for neighbors.

Oreena graduated high school, took some college courses but lost interest, instead working various odd jobs, including running errands, but now mostly paid, cash only. As soon as she turned 18 she applied for a chauffer's license, then became a full-time taxi driver, learning streets, shortcuts, tricks of the trade throughout the greater Detroit area. Saturdays were best, when she worked from four in the afternoon until about three Sunday morning. Drunks and party people tipped well, although on occasion they urinated or threw up in the taxi. She kept it up, driving at least fifty hours a week, until she turned twenty-one. She continued living with her parents, contributing well to the household expenses, but also banking as much as she could of the remainder.

Her next step, at twenty-one, was to obtain a commercial driver's license so she could leave the city streets and drunks behind and roll down the highway; this required attending a local truck driving school while continuing to drive taxis in the off hours. She faced a choice of paying her own way through the classes, or getting tuition support from a trucking firm, with the commitment to then drive for that company for several years or be required to pay back the tuition assistance. Oreena wanted the freedom to choose her employer, and so paid the tuition from her savings.

Once she graduated Oreena Jones applied for positions driving eighteen-wheelers, but found it hard to get into the truck-driving world. Her first job was package delivery in Detroit, but she kept trying to get into the big rigs. Finally a small firm, owned by a husband-wife team who still occasionally did the driving themselves, gave her the opportunity. She did some test runs with the female owner in the passenger seat, was hired, then started with day runs to Saginaw, Kalamazoo, Toledo. After six months she started taking loads into Canada, usually taking the Ambassador Bridge to access highways through the eastern portion of that country.

Membership in the LCTU, the Lorry, Carriage, and Truckers Union, was of course a given. Oreena found she liked the union meetings; she was not the woman driver, just a driver, just another member with stories to tell, speed traps to alert and complaints to beef about. She became active, helped with union activities and in seven years became president of the Greater Detroit chapter.

For three years Oreena worked as an independent contract driver pushing eighteen-wheelers down the road while continuing her union responsibilities, often making cell phone calls from rest stops and writing notes in a memo book she kept next to her when on the road. Her income dropped because she so often had to advise or intervene in situations where drivers had disputes with employers or contractors—disputes over sick leave, bonuses, discipline, but the work was stimulating; she so enjoyed the problem-solving side of her work.

One Monday she received a call from the Washington headquarters. Such calls weren't uncommon, but usually were concerning membership, dues, or a negative or positive incident that had made national news. This time was different.

"Hello, Oreena, its Doris. How are you, how things going?"

"Hey there Doris. Just fine. How's Simon? Nap time?"

"Nope, working hard. In fact, that's why I'm calling. He wants you to come to Washington, wants a meeting."

"OK, what's wrong?"

"Nothing, I assure you. Really. Just wants an important chat with you, rather not over the phone. Are you driving this week?"

"Short hop Wednesday, nothing Thursday, was planning on spending the day at the hall, clean up some business. But I can push that back till Friday or the weekend. How much time we talking about?"

"Union plane for you at the Detroit airport, North Terminal. Pick you up Thursday at nine, you'll be back in Detroit by mid-afternoon."

"Union plane? Never had that honor. Never even seen it. Do I get any hints about what's this about?"

"Another nope. Looking forward to seeing you, been a while."

When Oreena arrived at LCTU headquarters Doris Rosen greeted her warmly, then took her directly into Simon Drake's office, where he also gave her a warm, effusive greeting. "Welcome, Oreena, flight OK?"

"Sure Simon, flight was OK. A little weird, just me and a, what are they called now, flight attendant, and pilots I assume, didn't see them. Good coffee. But I'm guessing you didn't fly me here to small talk. Yes? Wait, actually, coffee getting to me, ladies' room first, then conversation."

When Oreena returned she found coffee, orange juice, scones waiting for them both.

"OK, Oreena, enough with the mystery. I'll be quick. I want you to become president of LCTU district five. Tom's going to retire in six weeks. He's been thinking about it for two years, finally pulled the thread. Gonna miss him; he's done a fine job. I need the fine job to continue. I need you."

A pause. "You want me to be president of the district?"

"I do. We do, the board agrees. You know the states, right?"

"Sure Michigan, Ohio, Pennsylvania, Indiana."

"That's the list. Yes we want you, no one more qualified, more experienced. And you've done a great job in Detroit." Now it was his turn to pause, she waited. "Of course this means you stop driving, just too much to do. There are some companies without unions we want to make a run at, at least two that have another union that, in our opinion, aren't doing a great job for the members, maybe we could pick them up, add them. Other side same coin, we have a few weak chapters, leadership in disarray or missing, we might lose them to de-unionization or to another union. Makes my stomach hurt to even say those words. So much to do. We can talk salary, but I assure you you'll make more than you are driving. Maybe not a ton more, but more, and no more diner food. Unless you like diner food."

"I do, won't give it up. Sounds like I'll be able to leave a bigger tip."

Simon tilted his head, smiled. "Did I just hear a yes?"

"Yes."

"So . . . You've read about the test, the national test of the driverless trucks, and about the debate in Congress, yes?"

"Of course. We all have. Lots of conversation about it, but kinda out of our hands, yah know? Big decisions by high-level folks, for sure. I'm assuming the union is weighing in, lobbying, right? I'm surprised you, we, haven't said anything, issued a statement."

"Believe me, Oreena, we are sure going to. Staff and board all looking at it, but we don't want to jump too early, come out on the wrong side of this. Bottom line is save jobs. Save truck driver jobs, keep them in the cab. We've got Representative Josiah Williams, I know you know Joe, we've got him on our side, pitching hard, but we're up against the trucking firms that want to boot out the drivers, run those rigs down the road without anyone home. They win; we're almost out of business. Not quite, but not representing drivers anymore except local, some other folks, some other fields, maybe do more janitorial union work, means taking them away from other unions . . . sorry, rambling. Back to bottom line. Save truck-driving jobs. Somehow. Gotta do it. Glad you're coming on board, sorry it is such a crappy time."

CHAPTER SIXTEEN

oger Kroggen, a registered D.C. lobbyist, represents the Consolidated Shippers and Freighters of America, the CSFA, an organization made up of the largest trucking companies. As their representative he advocates for lower taxes on diesel fuel, lower fees for apportioned license plates, use of double trailers, maximum weight per vehicle for various states and highways, regulations regarding hours of driving allowed per driver and similar matters. He regularly meets with the members of the House Committee on Transportation and Infrastructure, and as possible with staff of the Secretary of Transportation.

Once the text of the speech Josiah Williams made supporting house bill one one four was published, Roger Kroggen's cell phone started ringing, no surprise to him. He answered the callers, CEOs or COOs of his clients, with assurances that a counter argument would be made in the House, it was just a matter of who would give it; there were many members of Congress who were supportive of the CSFA. The trick was to find one who would benefit from the financial support of campaigns but would not risk losing tens of thousands of votes from angry truck drivers, their families and friends. So representatives of major ports or trucking centers such as Atlanta, Chicago, Oakland and others with numerous terminals and thousands of employees—and their families—tied to the trucks-with-drivers terminals would not be good candidates. No, the best was someone from a major financial center, a city where capital investment and the maximum utilization of assets was of utmost importance, but where those assets, if they involved human labor, were in other communities. The community that best fit that description was right there, near where he worked in Washington D.C. Numerous banks, investment houses with multiple millionaire and billionaire clients, real estate limited liability corporations with holdings around the world, but few dock workers, truck drivers, workers in the shipping and delivery industries. The wealthy suburbs of Maryland, just outside the capital, were perfect.

Roger knew that any representative he approached would have to be thoroughly familiar with the facts, have good, solid points of persuasion to counter the passionate speech of Representative Williams, which had received good press coverage across the nation and was picked up by all the news networks. But the counter-argument couldn't be based on passion, but rather on verifiable information, facts, logic. That meant a meeting with Frank Stevenson, at a location where the press was not likely to be present, and no one would alert them. He knew the Representative he wanted, Lance Whitford, a man firmly established in Maryland economics and politics, and a member of the Townehome Country Club, where a discreet meeting could be held, often was.

"Mr. Stevenson, this is US Representative Lance Whitford. Thank you for taking my call. Here's the reason . . . "

"I'm guessing it has something to do with my company's technology."

"Yes. Do you know about Representative Josiah William's house bill one one four, and his speech on the house floor?"

"Read it, memorized a few parts. 'Careening down our roads.' Gotta say, he did a good job of stating his case, stirring up scares. I should probably tell you, full disclosure, since his speech I've had the pleasure of meeting with Representative Williams in Washington, invited him to visit our shop, which he did, got to see our technology at work."

"Thank you for that. Sir, I've been approached by some private sector representatives who believe that your product is, to use an overused expression, one whose time has come. I am prepared to take a stand opposite Josiah's, but I need to be solid in my facts. Rock solid, and I'd like a thorough briefing from you, as much time as you need. I apologize, but there's no way I can fly to California and meet with you without the press being all over it, telling the world we're meeting. So I'm asking you to fly here, we'll meet at a country club whose staff I trust to not talk to any nosy reporters. I certainly know this is a busy time for you. . ."

"That's a serious understatement."

"Understood. But if you can carve out three days—I'm including travel—I'll give you undivided attention. Anything you want, video display, whiteboard, you name it. And you can send me documents by a secure line; we'll print what you need. Or bring flash drives. I'll have two of my staff with me. Help me ask good questions. I've got some great, smart folks."

The meeting took place two weeks later, at Townehome. They met for five hours, food ever present and plenty of juice and coffee. At the end of the time Representative Whitford felt he was ready to counter HB one one four; he needed to review, memorize some facts, but he had the information, the rebuttals, he needed.

CHAPTER SEVENTEEN

Simon Drake scheduled a meeting. In attendance were his top advisors and the district presidents, including the fairly new president Oreena Jones. The meeting started at nine, with instructions they were not to be disturbed unless it was a personal emergency; calls received by Doris Rosen and passed on as appropriate.

Simon began the meeting. "Ever since the driverless national test was announced I'm getting calls from drivers all over the country saying we should strike. Hell, even from California and Alaska at eight thirty, early morning their time, but wanted to make sure I got the message before they hit the road. I'm guessing you're all getting similar." The group nodded as one. Oreena added "I'm hearing from folks who think it is time for a strike, shutdown, maybe the whole country. Show America how important drivers are, like that."

"What do you tell them?" Simon asked.

"That we, the union, we are looking at the whole situation, of course want to protect their jobs, but we're pretty sure a strike isn't the best way to deal with this, this situation. I say that making it hard for folks to get their groceries and garden supplies on time might work against us, not sure America will see it our way. If they are just hot and swearing I ask for some time, call me in a week. Of course that was before you scheduled this meeting. Now I can tell them the leadership is meeting, planning, give us some time. I also let them know they've been heard." That got murmurs and comments of agreement around the table. "You know, they aren't all hotheads. Understandable, the heat that is. You should hear the talk, the fear. Sorry—I know all of you have. But there are a few, what should I call them, kinda the difference between 'we should strike' and 'do you think we should strike?' So for the drivers who ask that, if we should, what do I think, I tell them to think about the economics, the public image. What's that term, the optics? Optics, sounds like an eye exam. So with them, those who want to discuss, not just yell, I give them my honest opinion, the sour optics of a strike."

No one said anything, Simon encouraging her to continue with a gesture.

"Okay, first thing, what they want isn't possible, can't be a deal. I never say that, never try to lay hard reality on them when they are venting all over me, bitching would be a good term I guess . . . but here's the, yah, hard reality. No way in hell the trucking firms are going to put all those gadgets on their trucks, spend that money, and then pay a driver to ride along at full paycheck. Don't drive, just sit there, get paid full ride. Nope, not happening. It is one of two things; sit in the cab at a lower paycheck, maybe much lower, or be gone. Robots drive, drivers walk. Gone. The folks calling me don't want to hear that, but some day they will have to. Guess we'll have to see what Congress decides. Hey, I'm hogging the floor, enough?"

"You're doing fine, Oreena. We'll all get a chance, but is that it, anything else you tell those callers? I'm thinking this could help all of us." Nods of agreement and comments of encouragement followed.

"Okay, one more thing, something else I don't say but sure could happen. This is about drivers sitting in the robot trucks, not driving, getting paid. Already got the answer, the model. Some years ago, around '07 or '08, the automakers told the unions they were going to close some plants because the labor costs were too high. Go make them in Mexico or China or South Dumpstan, maybe Vietnam or some other world-end place. What the suits worked out was a half cut for the new hires. No change for those on the payroll, but about half that wage for anybody in the door after the contract was signed. Big, big savings for the suits, jobs saved but smaller paychecks for anybody hired after that date, so not near the factory floor earnings as before. Boss goes to the union with that deal. Well it sucked from the employees' point of view, but of course they had to accept it. Accept it or the jobs all go to South Dumpstan. So now the same for this, except if a cut in pay isn't accepted for the new kids then the robots just take over, no jobs at all."

Simon added "Yes, I don't see Congress passing a law saying truckers in all the cabs, no cuts, all paid full freight. Not going to happen. Thanks, Oreena, that's helpful, clear."

The district president from the far Midwest, stationed in Lincoln, Nebraska, asked if Oreena, or Simon, or anyone, had a guess on what Congress would be doing.

Oreena shrugged. Simon answered, "We will have robot trucks. Not going to stop that, no way. And, sad and sorry to say, probably someday no human in most of the tractor cabs. Very sorry to say, but I see that coming. How do we get there? Oreena's discussion of the auto industry was right, but I don't see that happening, that is, we keep drivers forever but new hires get paid, say, half. If the technology is really as good as I'm guessing it will be, drivers are gone. Gone, all robots. Not tomorrow, not the next day, but some day, and not all that many years. And so, my friends, a strike is an empty gesture. At best . . . hells bells, I can't think of a best. The worst is all it does is piss off the entire country, food deliveries late and a thousand other problems and Congress acts quicker and maybe meaner, punitive."

The man from Nebraska nodded, responded. "I agree. I just don't see any upside to a strike. There aren't enough union workers in America any more, we wouldn't have a lot of brothers and sisters cheering us on. And the first question is how long. A one or two-day strike would only inconvenience people, piss them off, cost the drivers some wallet money, but not move Congress or lawmakers to change their minds. A longer strike would cost the drivers money, food would rot, we'd be seen as stopping progress *and* driving up inflation at the same time. Not a good parlay."

Silence around the table. Finally Simon spoke. "So what does Oreena, what do you all say when your phones ring as soon as you get back in the office? Here's my suggestion, something like we don't make the laws but we're working with Congress, we hear you, we hear them all, but we can't make any promises because . . . repeating myself, we don't make the laws."

They spent four more hours in discussion, planning on lobbying efforts with their members of Congress, appropriating funds for television ads if necessary, getting agreement about talking points to members and the public.

Frank Stevenson called the Reed brothers, asked them to come for a meeting. They joined him as before, in his office, this time with coffee available along with juice and cookies. He greeted Paul and Henry warmly.

"Welcome, thanks for coming on short notice. We've received approval for a national test, no date set yet but going to happen soon. We'd like to use one of your trucks. Here's the reason; we don't want critics saying that GeeCee is a special truck, different from other eighteen-wheelers on the road. I mean, let me say that better . . . of course it will have the T O T cameras and radar, the electronics, but aside from that it us just a normal big rig. If people are told, or just believe, that it isn't normal, then we lose credibility. So let's put T O T on one of your trucks, an older one, scratches and stains, showing its age, at least a hundred and fifty thousand on the engine. Of course we'll check the engine, tires, shocks, make sure it is as reliable as possible, don't want an embarrassing breakdown. But your truck, your logo on it—we'll tell the world how old it is, how many miles, make the point that T O T can go on any rig. Make it loud and clear."

"Sure, we've got those" Paul answered. "Two of them with engines somewhere around a hundred eighty, some good scratches on the cabs. Hell, if you want we can add a few."

"I'm curious, really not my business but I'm wondering what you've told your drivers about BQD's involvement, about adding T O T."

Henry answered. "We've been putting it off, but have to do it now. Now. And we're still hoping you'll work with us, carry the paper for the first two. Let's us carefully control our cash flow, not get too deeply in debt."

"Happiness definition is positive cash flow" Paul added.

"Yep. So we're going to start with two trucks, then add one a year to our present six trucks. If all goes well we'll hook up faster. It would be nice to have all six trucks T O T-equipped in five years. Optimistic, ten to twelve fully equipped trucks in ten years."

Frank nodded his approval. "Certainly we can carry the paper, just have to work out the payment plan, something you two can work with, not too much pressure on your cash flow. Oh, and reasonable interest, say . . . Twenty-five percent?"

Both brothers stared at him. Frank hastened to continue. "Zero interest. I just can't tell a joke, should quick trying."

The Reed brothers asked their drivers to come to a meeting on a Sunday, giving people two weeks to plan the schedule. They promised the drivers no more than two hours plus a three hundred dollar payment for their troubles; it was critical to have all drivers present.

Henry began the meeting. "Thank you all for coming. We said two hours, and we'll stick to that promise, maybe shorter; depends on what questions you have, which we'll be glad to answer. Okay, here's what's up. We are going to contract with a company called MHR. They make a system, called Transportation Operation Technology, T O T, where the truck is driven without a driver, that is, computers drive the truck. No doubt you've read about, heard about it." The announcement was met with hard faces, stony silence. "We, Paul and I, want you to know we care about you, want to make this transition as easy as possible. We have a plan to do that." The faces stayed hard, with a hint of anger showing.

Paul took over. "The first thing to tell you is that the total transition is going to take time, years. Soon we will be equipping two trucks; one will be used in a national test. Over time, additional trucks. The second thing is that whatever we can do to make the transition as easy as possible for you we'll do. Whatever you decide—stay with us for years, driving for a new firm, changing careers, retiring, whatever you want to do, we'll help."

Phil, one of the drivers, spoke up. "I might be one of those early retire-ment folks, depending on what you're offering. What?"

Paul responded. "Let's do this, Phil. Henry or I will schedule a pri-vate meeting with you and everyone else who wants one. We can start those next Monday. If you're on the road we can meet in the evening, on the weekends, whatever works best for you. Again, we want so much for this to be as little a disruption as possible in your lives, maybe a good next step. And it won't be right away, in fact we're looking at months before the test."

Phil persisted. "So who gets screwed out of a truck first?"

"Actually, no one. MHR wants to show companies that they don't have to put their equipment on a newer truck, that any diesel, long-haul rig can accept it. So it will be one of ours with at least one-fifty on it, so you know which two are most likely. While it is being set up we will replace it with a leased cab. As I said, this all takes time. Time to equip the truck, time to agree with the feds on a national test, and then run that test. And then there's a little shop called Congress that just might weigh in with some rules and regulations."

CHAPTER EIGHTEEN

In the middle of the warehouse district in Detroit, Michigan, a few blocks from where Clark Street ends at West Jefferson Avenue, sits the 3433, a diner that opened in the 1940s and became a twenty-four hour diner in the early 1960s, opening at 3:00 a.m. Monday morning and serving until 2:00 p.m. Saturday afternoon, breakfast served anytime. Standard diner menu; eggs, pancakes, mounds of fried potatoes, club and BLT and roast beef with gravy and ham and cheese sandwiches, steaks and chops. Good, hearty coffee, orange juice, pop, water. No alcohol. No cappuccinos.

By far most of the customers were drivers. Next to the diner were parked panel vans, pickups, freezer trucks, a variety of delivery vehicles, the occasional car. The 3433 purchased additional land twenty years ago and could now park ten bobtails in the next lot.

The clientele was usually all drivers and helpers, especially before 7:00 a.m. Toward the back of the restaurant, near the kitchen door, was an eight-top with a sign on it

RESERVED
LONG-HAUL DRIVERS ONLY

Drivers would meet each other and chat. They would see a friend, or friendly acquaintance, once every other month or so or maybe a year apart, depending how their schedules matched up; thus the table held a mixture of two or three or eight drivers, some of whom had never met, some who had met four times in the past three years; an ever-changing cast of characters. But conversation, if wanted, came easy, talking about the LCTU, highway patrols, rest stops and truck stops and speed limits and federal and state regulations and inspections and sharing jokes. On occasion one of the drivers was a woman; she easily parried the remarks she'd heard a thousand times but was accepted as one of the group because, in fact, she was.

Kyle Braxton was about to dig into a breakfast of chopped steak, hash browns, sourdough toast, eggs, and—because his wife insisted he do so—a small fruit bowl. Black coffee. He took a few bites and then began. "So here's the deal. I'm forty-seven. My brother-in-law does my . . . our taxes. Smart dude. So he tells me that the best is, if my body will stand it, drive till I'm sixty-five. Keeps stressing about my body, says dying behind the wheel will cut into my retirement plans. Him and his sister, my dear wife . . . see, I'm eating the damn fruit! So like I'm say-ing, if I can keep chugging till sixty-five, the company retirement plus social security, the wife and me, we're in good shape. She could retire at sixty-two or sixty-five, something we could talk about, but it's like that. I don't want to fuck it up, don't want nothin' to fuck it up. Eat my damn fruit, drive to sixty-five."

He paused ate a few moments, but aside from a few small comments the other four men at the table waited, sensing more was coming.

Kyle continued. "Now along comes this gadget, this automatic driver shit. I know that we all think we can outdrive any machine. So did John Henry. But look at modern electrical stuff—hell, look at this!" he said, pulling out his cell phone. "Takes damn good pictures, phones around the world, tells me the weather here or anywhere I'm driving to, compass, calculator, news updates, traffic updates—that one, that highway bulletins app has kept me out of a bunch of jams, shows alter-nate routes—I mean, all that in something that weighs about what a sandwich does. This model you can have at the sink while you're shav-ing, drop it in the water you just pull it out and wipe it off, keep shaving. No problem. How the hell they do that? So don't be saying it can't be done, can't have a truck get from here to Louisville or Atlanta without a driver. Piece of cake for the techie boys. Couldn't peddle my rig if their life depended on it, but that's not the point. Point is it can be done, is being done."

A driver with an I'm Steady Truckin! cap pulled low over his eyes said "They gotta be stopped."

Kyle looked at him. Like many of the meetings at this table the drivers didn't know each other well, having met perhaps a few times in recent years. "A, they can't be stopped. They go ahead with this and there will be thousands of rigs with the wires on them inside four, five years. Thousands. You gonna drive up and down the highways with wire cutters? Or maybe you're thinking shotguns or some damn gun thing, your buddy drives and you shoot. Brilliant idea, brilliant. You'll have your ass in jail for the rest of your life or you'll be so old when you get out it won't matter. Last pussy you have before getting busted will be last you ever get. Or, if you're lucky, some highway patrol dude will blow your damn head off. Your business, my man, not mine. Not going there. Gonna retire and sit on my front porch and spoil my grandkids with the good monthlies I've got coming in." Kyle paused, stretched his head back, winced. "I don't resent growing old, I get it, people live and die. Not much any of us can do about it. But what I'm not happy about is what aches and pains mean to me now, different from what they used to mean."

"Meaning. . . ."

"Younger, it meant I lifted something wrong or it was an honorable sports injury or some shit like that. Now, I'm thinking, wondering, if it is the first sign of heart problems, liver failing, the big C. Get a poking pain, a strange twitch, and I'm thinking soon I'll be in the hospital surrounded by loving relatives."

Steady Truckin responded, his voice up a bit. "You can forget all that spoiling grandkids bullshit, won't have no fucking good monthlies. They gonna empty the cab and tell you to have a nice day, don't you get it?"

"Man, I'm as pissed as you. I'm there with you, no argument. But we got us a powerful union, and we can make things happen in D.C. I'm guessing we'll settle out with a rule that says there has to be a driver. . . ."

"Just sitting there" said Steady Truckin derisively. "Picking my nose and scratching my ass. And getting paid for it."

Another of the group of five spoke up for the first time. His choice of cap wear was the 3433 logo. "But it won't be the same pay. Can't be the same pay and pay off for the bosses. Third cut, half cut?"

Another derisive snort from Steady Truckin. "No way that goes down. We'll walk, shut down the country. Hell, we all know the numbers. Seventy percent of freight moves by truck. Seventy percent! I mean, teddy bears and radios and televisions, and how about the life stuff? Food, my friends. Food!"

Kyle, chewing a hearty mouthful, shook his head sadly.

"What?"

"You ever looked at our contract, really read it? I have, a few times. Here's the deal, plain and simple. They got work, they have to offer it to you first. Can't go hire somebody new and plug him into your truck. Seniority, that's the magic word. But what if they offer it to you, and you say no, and the next man says no, and the next . . . till the end of the line. Know what? Then they can go out and hire. And they can offer that new man half of what you get."

"But pay is set in the contract . . . "

Kyle nodded yes, mopped up the last of his eggs with the last of his toast. He sighed a bit and finished the fruit bowl, then reached for his coffee. "New contract. That's what they're going to do. Either bust the union or get it to agree that all new drivers come in at half of what we make. I'm guessing they'll work a deal with us old farts, maybe grandfather us same pay, but as the years go by the old go out and the new come in at half-price. Union wants to stay in the game, keep power in D.C. and those hot-shit fine offices, they'll work out a deal. They choose to fight to the end, no compromise, no deal, they lose. It'll end."

Kyle leaned back, enjoying his professorial role. The others were paying close attention. "I've been doing some serious reading since this hit the news. Two things. First is that I've read our union book again. Read up on unions, too. I'm sure you guys know this like I do, but the hard numbers are, well, hard. You go way back to the days when the UAW and AFL-CIO and the mineworkers, the UMWA, and our beloved LCTU were the bitches, mid-nineteen fifties had a good thirty-five percent of workers. Days long gone, my brothers, long gone. We're lucky to keep above one of ten. Almost all teachers, security guards, government folks, scattering of others, some cops, and of course truckers. And coal miners, a shrinking group. All of 'em in a bunch, one in ten.

He paused, others sitting listening. One looked at his watch, shrugged, kept sitting at the table; this was too important to walk away from. Kyle continued "There's something else going on. Another aspect to this, gotta think about it. There aren't enough of us. Just not near enough drivers hauling ass. Hell, how many of us company drivers have 'Help Wanted, We Pay More' or some similar shit on the back of our rigs. One reason the driver demand is so high, and keeps being high, is that we've got all these trailers, nearly six million of them, and about two million bobtails ready to hook them up. Lots of demand for us driver folks." He paused, the others waited. "So I'm talking to my wife about it, how being in demand gives us leverage, power, you see what I mean? My smart wife, lucky me for sure, she points out it is a, what you call that, a two-edge sword?"

"Yeah, or double-edge, or edged. Sorry. Just messing with you" said another of the drivers.

"Hey, my wife fixes my English, won't ever let me say ain't. Join the parade."

"OK, do it, will you? What's the other edge?"

"The fact that we have a shortage, always a shortage, all around the country, means they have to treat us right, cut us some slack when we—what—miss a day or screw up the paperwork, and for sure pay us, pay us fat city or as close as the union can push them. But that's only so long as the owners need drivers. They need us, we have power, they don't, we lose power. So how do we lose? What if the owners don't need us, things get to the point where they never have to recruit? Don't have to hire, don't have to pay benefits, don't have to fight with the union? Think about that, my hard-working friends . . . what if the owners don't need drivers? What my wife lays on me is that the other side of the driver shortage giving us, you know, power, clout, is that the owners are hotter than hell to get rid of us. If there were lots of us, oversupply kinda, the damn replacement machines wouldn't be such a big deal. But this shortage is, as she says, pushing the machines into the owner's arms."

Eric Suda, who took over the Detroit region of the LCTU when Oreena was promoted, called her and asked for a meeting, which was swiftly granted.

"Thanks for seeing me right away, Oreena. I appreciate it."

"Sure. How's the new job going? Starting to feel right?"

"No, not yet, just because it takes a while to see things from this side, from the 'run the union' side rather than as a member. Instead of wanting the union to do stuff for me, now I'm the yodel who does that stuff. Shift of viewpoint, but hell, you know what I mean, you been where I am a few years back."

"Yes, a shift in viewpoint. I like the way that sounds. So . . . "

"O, I've got a lot of hot members. Between you and me, scared members. So the whole damn picture; angry, scared, worried, a real mess. Phone calls and emails and folks showing up at the hall nonstop."

"About the driverless trucks."

"Ready to walk. Worse, ready to tie up traffic, create a hell of a mess, show their power, how important they are."

"Think about that. I mean, sorry, get those drivers to think about that. Robots never go on strike, never tie up traffic because they're pissed at the bosses or government or some shit. All that would do is make them want those robots more, sooner. And that ain't the worst. The worst is that Congress tells us all to shove it, approves those robots so fast your head spins. Eric, tell them not to do it!"

"I'll try, O, I'll try. Got your point, but they might not be listening."

Eric Suda tried, but the desire by his members to do something, something!, overcame him and his—and Oreena's—logic. Five days

later six trucks started the climb on the Ambassador Bridge, maneu-
vering to be three in a row in each lane, side by side. At that point the
drivers shut off the engines and sat there. They knew that walking back
down the bridge was pointless, partly because behind them it was all
major highways, customs, control points, no place to have a car waiting,
idling—and partly because in less than a minute there were bridge staff
and law officers on the scene. All six submitted to arrest but refused to
hand over their keys; it wasn't until they were booked that the keys were
recovered and the trucks started up and backed down the ramps. The
tie-up was tremendous and terrible, taking the better part of twenty-four
hours before traffic moved normally again.

CHAPTER NINETEEN

An agreement was finally reached about the national test. It would start from the Bakersfield home and head north. Unannounced, to prevent traffic jams, there would be exits to put GeeCee on small roads, county two-lane routes, and on occasion leave marked routes to drive on small country lanes, perhaps roads showing neglect; crumbling shoulders and potholes. Some portion would be at night.

The MHR staff knew GeeCee, their technology, was ready for a national test, not a secret run but one covered by the press and of course by the federal highway administration; no doubt the LCTU would want to be part of the process, and perhaps Representative Williams and other members of Congress. Frank Stevenson called Stewart Timmerlee. "Stewart, we're ready. We're inviting your administration to put our technology to the test. You design it, we'll run it, although you may get input from others. . . . "

"Asked for or not."

"Yes, but we raise no objections as long as it is reasonable. I'd rather not be asked to drive across a sand dune or through six feet of water, but anything that a big rig might run into is fair game. Night, rain, detour signs, all good. Do it.

"Fine. We will notify the LCTU, have to, they'll bitch if we don't give them a chance to help design the test. And the rep who objected, made that 'careening down our roads' speech.... and anyone else who has a reasonable claim to a seat at the table."

"Our thinking is to have a winding route from Bakersfield, north, not all major roads; we want to get on some small country roads, county routes maybe, but narrow, tight is good. A real test. Have our driver spend the night, security of course, then get up way before dawn, do some deep dark driving. And detour signs. And other . . . challenges, tests. Hard, demanding, that's what we want, so there is demonstrated proof in the capabilities of the technology. Oh, something else. A small company, six trucks, family owned company, approached us about being the first to be equipped. We're going to use one of their trucks, a well-worn diesel with over a hundred fifty-thousand on it."

"To demonstrate the system can be installed on an older truck, right?"

"Exactly."

The National Highway Traffic Safety Administration has an important but strictly professional relationship with the Lorry, Carriage, and Truckers Union. The administration puts forth regulations, such as hours of required rest, to protect the drivers and the public. The LCTU works to allow truckers to earn a living with only absolutely necessary rules, regulations, advisories. Many debates, in private and in leaks to the media, are held over differing definitions of 'absolutely necessary.'

Stewart called Simon. "Simon, thanks for taking my call. I understand you're familiar with the electronic support known as T O T, the technology that can handle some driving chores."

"Or eliminate all driving chores, all drivers."

Stewart moved the phone away from his mouth, briefly sighed, then continued. "Simon, you know my job. Someone comes to us with something that might impact highway operations and safety we have to look at it. Anti-skid pavement, proposed different lighting systems or signage, we review it, make a decision on its acceptability. Yes, Simon, this could impact jobs. That's for you and the learned members of Congress to hash out. I'm just the guy with the microscope."

"Accepted. So you're calling because . . . "

"We are going ahead with a national test of the . . . that is, a test this administration is supervising. The manufacturers, T O T folks, are going to give us the basics, the outline of a route, and some challenges. Depending on what they say we will add on; they understand we're going to augment the challenges. What I'm offering you, offering your union, is a chance to provide input on the test. What would you like to have it do, perform? What hoops to jump through? That really stretches the metaphor . . . jumping trucks."

"Will the trailer be empty?"

"No, that wouldn't be a fair test. For stability and to make the run realistic, the truck will be loaded with fifteen tons of cement blocks on pallets. I know that's below the legal limit, but this isn't a test of the trailer, it's about the system, and our truck experts say that would be a fair test of road handling and braking."

"Thank you. That weight is fine, yes, I agree, fair test." Simon paused. "Can I get back to you? I've got some ideas, night driving, detours, that kind of thing, but that might already be planned by the company. Tell you what. Let me know what you and they come up with, let us see if there is something we want to add. Depends on how tough, rigorous, it is. We might add to the test, might not."

Three days later Simon called back. "Stewart, thank you for allowing us to provide input on the test. The LCTU appreciates it."

"You're certainly welcome. It's proper, appropriate. So what do you have in mind?"

"Three things. Dark night, no moonlight, out in the country, just plain dark. A small country road, and a turn onto another small country road. So, a tight corner in the middle of nowhere—no lights except the truck's."

"We're actually planning on all that already, so . . . "

"And ice."

"Ice?"

"Yep. How does the machine handle an icy road. Our drivers know what to do, will the machine? That is our request."

"And we will comply. Adds a logistical wrinkle we weren't planning on, but wrinkle we will. Ice. You've got it. Thank you."

"Good. Now when the test takes place, who will see it? And what will they be seeing? And can I be one of those watching?"

"Absolutely, Simon. Whether the LCTU designed part of the test or not, we would have invited you to watch. So . . . the answer is there will be people in the highway administration, some reporters, some trucking firm owners, probably lawyers and police or highway patrol. Invitation list still to be determined, but about like that. All on a closed loop, a code needed to access."

"That sounds like I can watch this nighttime test from the comfort of my home."

"Sure, but remember the test will be in California, so it won't be so monster early for you, Washington time."

"Okay, and . . . oh, Stewart, one more question. You said reporters. Won't every reporter want to cover this? How are you going to handle that crowd?"

"We're going to do it like they do presidential press conferences, some kind of press pool. Draw straws or some damn thing, haven't figured it out yet, but likely some reporters in California, Washington, maybe Chicago, watching on a big screen together. Of course clips will be made available for the TV folks, evening news. Actually, earlier news, right?"

They thanked each other for the cooperation, hung up. Stewart Timmerlee mentally acknowledged that one of the lucky straws drawn would go to James Dorfmann.

CHAPTER TWENTY

It was the day of the national test. Photographers, James Dorfmann among them, were crowded around the gate and ready to follow, but the number was limited to three specific, identified vehicles. The local police and highway patrol had been alerted and were determined to keep control of the situation, to not allow cars going back and forth around the truck, jockeying for position, and any staying with the truck that was not one of the three would be pulled over; this was made clear through emails to the media and a newspaper announcement. A lieutenant in the Bakersfield police and a deputy from the Kern County sheriff made the rounds of the waiting drivers, issuing stern warnings about following too closely or repeatedly racing ahead of the truck and creating hazards. Although the drivers weren't told, a sheriff's plane would follow and report until the truck left the county, and the highway patrol would also fly over at least part of the route, reporting to waiting officers below.

The Bakersfield True Press was of course one of the news sources permitted to be part of the California press pool. Jakub Billski was going to be the representative, and he would coordinate with his friend James to put together the local coverage, with pictures, that would appear online and in print.

GeeCee emerged from the warehouse doors at eight a.m., Ellen unsmiling, calm behind the wheel while not touching it or the gears or pedals; inside cab cameras were trained on her hands and feet, broadcasting to anyone who wanted to watch. Everyone referred to the truck as GeeCee, although it actually was a BQD tractor and trailer.

After a while many turned off the broadcast because there was nothing to see except two unmoving hands and two unmoving feet, plus the outside camera views, normal scenes familiar to any driver of cars or trucks. Among those who watched, kept watching, took notes, were Simon Drake and his staff, Oreena Jones and the other LCTU district presidents, a few government officials.

In the first hundred feet from the warehouse were photographers, photos non-stop as the truck approached and passed the waiting cameras. Most of the photographers then got into waiting vehicles, but a deputy sheriff cruised about five car lengths behind the truck, and attentive officers in highway patrol cars sat in medians, so the parade of vehicles soon, as planned, disbanded, and the truck rolled on north, followed by only the three approved vehicles.

One of those who continued to follow was James Dorfmann. He sat in the passenger seat, camera in his lap, having convinced a neighbor to take a day off and be paid to be his driver. James took pictures from behind GeeCee, then they carefully passed the truck while James held down the camera's trigger in three-second bursts. They then drove several miles ahead so James could jump out and take pictures as GeeCee passed. All three continued to trail or pass and photograph, but the presence of numerous county and state patrol cars kept the followers well behaved.

The plan called for an early overnight in Eugene. While Ellen slept, three guards were posted near the truck, and Eugene police were on alert. Nothing occurred. Very early the next morning, two hours before dawn, the return home began. On the way, just north of the California border, the sky still dark, GeeCee left I-5 and headed toward a narrow two-lane country road, a link between farming communities. A moonless night; except for an occasional security light near farmhouses and barns there was only starlight. Dark, very dark. By agreement the road was blocked to traffic for one hour. As GeeCee approached a barrier there were no lights, just sawhorses with **ROAD CLOSED** reflective signs. Two garden hoses sprayed water into the air, the mock rain falling in a wide pattern on the sawhorses and the road before and beyond. The truck slowed, stopped twenty feet from the sawhorses, water splattering on the windshield.

Back in Bakersfield a yellow light turned on over the screens showing what GeeCee's cameras were seeing, and a soft *ping* sounded. This was a recent addition to the system, it alerted the wrangler—who, like Ellen, didn't know what was coming—that something unusual was happening, the wrangler should pay attention and be ready to assist. As was intended, the wrangler noticed the alert but did nothing, just waited. At that point a highway patrol officer emerged, dragged aside one of the barriers, and with a flashlight and hand signal indicated GeeCee should proceed. The truck started rolling slowly, followed the officer's signals, continued; the yellow light turned off. After a half-mile there was a detour sign, an arrow pointing to the right, requiring a turn onto another country road. For two hundred feet before the intersection and into it, and two hundred feet down the road to the right, were over a thousand pounds of crushed ice that had been offloaded and spread only an hour before. This part of the test was quite expensive; purchasing that much ice, crushed and stored in trucks, delivered and spread in the middle of the night, large work lights provided so well-paid workers could do the spreading, the lights turned off as the job was completed.

GeeCee's lights picked up something gleaming in the road ahead. Because the computer could not immediately identify it the truck began slowing. Ellen had not been told about any part of the test so as to preemptively head off challenges based on the human knowing in advance and somehow communicating with the truck. As the truck started to slow Ellen stared and then realized what she was seeing. Ice. And then a detour sign. For the first time since the initial run out of the Bakersfield warehouse, after many hundreds of miles of watching the T O T technology do what it did so well, she moved her right hand toward the switch that would give her instant control. Even at this hour she was awake and alert; ready to flip the switch but not really concerned, having spent so many hours seeing what T O T could do, comfortable with its abilities. Back in Bakersfield, for the second time in a few minutes, the yellow light and soft *ping* alerted the wrangler.

The eighteen-wheeler with its heavy load, alone on a small country road, in a moonless night, performed as the engineers, the programmers, had expected. It slowed, slowed to fifteen miles an hour, put on the right turn signal and slowed further, the automatic transmission downshifting as the cab swung a bit to the left and then started a right turn. At this point the speed was down to about five miles per hour. The turn was completed, the eighteen thousand pounds of the cab pressing down, the drive wheels slipping then gaining traction. The trailer came close to the right edge of the intersection, but because of that small left swing the wheels didn't come off the road. It continued on the ice-covered road at fifteen, driving straight, until the ice was in the rear view mirrors. Ellen sat back, smiled, thought about retiring, paying off everything, putting most of three hundred thousand in her pocket, starting a new life. She nodded her head, whispered "Thank you, GeeCee." She thought of something she heard a race driver say; "I cain't get no gription with muh tars." GeeCee got gription with its tars on the ice, moving as slowly as the conditions required. Ellen smiled again.

In the quiet of his den Simon Drake watched, saw GeeCee successfully navigate the water-hose rain and the icy turn that was broadcast to the restricted network, but what would be widely covered by television in the coming twenty-four hours. He said out loud to the empty room "So that's it. That's it."

CHAPTER TWENTY-ONE

After all the debates, the politicking, the lobbying, the pressure from unions and company owners and numerous interest groups the final outcome was that economics won. At the celebration of the national approval, an event where Frank Stevenson thanked everyone and announced the ten thousand dollar bonuses would be issued next week, he said "There are two things you can't beat—well, three if you include death, lots of folks beat taxes, but you can't beat gravity or supply and demand. In the end, despite all the posturing and shouting the economics of supply and demand won. In this case it is just simply that if I use the technology and don't have a driver then I can deliver goods cheaper than someone else can if they have a driver. That simple. Now I know this isn't the usual way that phrase supply and demand is applied, but this is demand and supply. You have to think of it as a demand for lower costs, for buying what you want to buy with fewer of your dollars, use fewer dollars to deliver goods. That's the demand, driverless trucks are the supply." He paused. "Think of it as a first cousin to necessity being the mother of invention. A necessity to deliver goods quicker, cheaper, with less waste was the mother of the freight train, the steamboat, the eighteen-wheeler, and now GeeCee."

One week after the completion of the national test, GeeCee, the modified BQD truck, was back in the Bakersfield warehouse. Additional land had been purchased, so in addition to the building, over thirty thousand square feet, there was now a large, fenced-in gravel parking lot, a fence topped with barbed wire that extended around the building, including an electronic gate. The space was far larger than needed for the electronic development work, so there was plenty of room to expand, take deliveries, park cars in a secure lot, the entire building surrounded by a high fence. There were two armed guards stationed outside, one at the gate, the other patrolling the perimeter in an electric cart. Cameras showed every inch of the property.

Frank had decided to give Stewart Timmerlee the week to discuss test results with his staff and plan the government's response. He was planning on calling that day or the next, but his phone rang at eight, soon after arriving for work. It was Frieda Shippens calling for Mr. Timmerlee, could Mr. Stevenson attend an eleven thirty meeting the following Monday, lunch would be served. He quickly agreed.

When Frank arrived the greetings were professional, quick and cordial. Both men knew this would be a critical few hours, and tension was in the air. They remained standing.

"Frank, we've got a hell of a situation, you and I. But I've been having a conversation that I think can move things forward. Before I go further, I need your pledge that all you will say is that the two of us reviewed the results of the test, talked about what happens next, didn't reach any firm conclusions. Further, I need you to pledge to tell a lie, that lie being—if you are asked—that there were only the two of us present. I'll release you from that pledge at some point, but not now. Sorry, I know that is a hard thing to hear, but I need it to . . . well, as I said, move things forward."

"Not to be too dramatic, but we both know this is a turning point in history. I understand, and you have my solemn promise. Glad to."

"Thank you." The administrator of the national highway traffic safety administration walked to a door across from the one Frank had come through. He opened it and said "Please come in."

A man entered. "Frank Stevenson, this is Simon Drake, president of the LCTU."

Frank stuck out his hand for a firm handshake. "This is a pleasure, Mr. Drake. I certainly know who you are. Thank you for meeting with me."

"Please, how about first names? And I hope you agree it is a pleasure two hours from now."

Frank smiled. Stewart invited them to sit at a six-person round conference table. Almost immediately staff entered with coffee, hot water for tea, juice and two small silver carafes of ice water, which were quickly and quietly set on a sideboard. When they were alone again Simon asked "There's a question I like to ask when I meet someone I'm going to work with, question being—Frank, do you know what LCTU stands for?"

Another smile from Frank. "The lorry, carriage, and truckers union. Some of the founders had fathers who were truck—lorry—drivers in England and other parts of the UK, or fathers or grandfathers who drove carriages in England or France or the early days here. It was about honoring the history of the trade. Sometime after world war two there was a movement to change the name, be more modern, came to a close vote at a national convention . . . nineteen fifty, fifty-five . . . . around there, but the traditionalists held out. You've got about a million and a half members in many occupations. How am I doing?"

Now it was Simon's turn to smile. "Done your homework. Not surprised. And it was the fifty-five convention. The whole thing was recorded, eventually transcribed. Lots of pages, it's the whole convention pretty much, but the pages with the arguments for and against change make for interesting reading. May I send you those?"

"Absolutely. Thank you."

Stewart was feeling beneficent, optimistic. "Lunch in fifteen minutes, gentlemen. Meanwhile, liquids of your choice. Maybe if we end well a toast with something else. You'll notice there's a lock on that sideboard."

Simon was dressed in a sport coat and tie. He took off the coat, unbuttoned his top shirt button and loosened his tie. Time for work. "Frank, here's where I am. Wait . . . thanks for agreeing to keep this confidential for now. I couldn't be here if you hadn't done that."

"Sure. In fact, don't send those pages until we go public. No links."

"Good thinking. Look, no surprise I've got folks yelling for a nationwide strike, all divisions, shut down the country. What they see is the short term, small picture. I don't blame them, I understand the worry, fear, anger . . . talking about putting a million truckers out of work! But I've got to see the big picture, the future of the union, Congress, the reaction of Americans. Shut down the nation? That'll earn us love. No food shipments, California and Florida citrus rotting . . . long, long list. Can't forget that close to ninety percent of hourly employees are not unionized. Don't like it, but that's America today, and I don't see it moving more than a bit up or down from there. And Congress . . . never mind. Anyway, we can't do that. Already have some calling for my head on a pike, dump me and elect a real leader. Like that."

Frank responded. "Simon, I have some good news for you. It contains a however, I'll come to that. But if you like it and we can reach a general agreement maybe our host will get out his key and unlock that little door. Wonder if he keeps it on a silver chain around his neck?"

That got general laughter. Frank too removed his jacket and loosened his button and tie, then leaned forward.

"When we started on this we thought it would be exactly that, drivers out of work, empty cabs up and down the highways. That's no longer our model, not right away. We expect Congress to come up with a compromise. My guess is it will be a mix of something like phasing out drivers over time, helping with retirement, maybe grandfather clause for those already on the payroll, special bonuses, early onto Social Security . . . I'm not holding out on you, no inside info, but it seems reasonable that's what they'll produce; that is, no requirement that there always has to be a driver, but some way to ease the loss of employment, or move to new employment. And over years, maybe a decade or more."

They were interrupted by a knock on the door, followed by staff bringing a selection of sandwiches in quarters; ham and cheese, roast beef, avocado with lettuce and tomato. Potato chips and pretzels. They asked what the three wanted to drink, served those beverages and left. The men filled their plates then continued.

Frank said "Let me add one more thing, it's important. It is when we decided that a driverless truck really wasn't a fantasy, we knew we had to have a way for a human to take control if needed. What we came up with, at great expense if I may complain for a moment, was a system where a person would, from our headquarters, see everything T O T sees. If the truck isn't sure what to do it alerts the . . . wrangler, we call them. Actually the system alerts the wrangler anytime something unusual is spotted. The neat thing is that the wrangler can actually drive the truck. You know those arcade games where you are driving a motorcycle or racecar? Similar. The wrangler sits in a full mock-up of the cab and drives the truck.

"Impressive" said Stewart. Simon sat silent.

Frank continued. "The software can easily interpret speed limit, detour, merge, similar signs. Stop signs and yield and red or green lights no problem. Cars, trucks, bicycles, motorcycles and scooters . . . we've got those covered, lots of tests, repeated tests, the trucks slow down, pull over, or alert a wrangler back in our control center—which is rare. A big hurdle, big development was that we couldn't be sure about reading correctly the directions given by an officer in the middle of the road. Someone waving an arm or flashlight, probably highway patrol or sheriff, you get the idea. So when the front system detects anyone in the road it reacts quicker than a human could, should do the right thing but also alerts the wrangler. T O T will slow, brake as needed . . . we did do some tests; rolled baby carriages in front of a slow moving vehicle, had robots the size of small children dart out, repeated those tests too, many times. Had folks pretend to be officers giving directions and the system alerted the wrangler. All this information compiled and updated constantly, at a minimum of twenty times per second."

"I've heard that before" said Simon "But it is still hard to grasp, twenty times a second. And I understand that's slow in today's computer world."

"Quite slow indeed" Frank answered "but plenty fast enough for this task. Already computers tell automatic transmissions to shift right on the spot, the perfect point, meaning even if it is only a hair better than a trained human, that means savings over the thousands of miles.

But now we are talking about perfectly safe driving, no trucks with time lost because they were pulled over for speeding, fewer accidents, eventually lower workers' comp rates and lowered insurance. That last one is big, big. As I'm sure you know, insurance costs trucking firms a ton."

Simon said "Is there another side to this, another view, or is it all just good news for the elimination of drivers? Sorry for the crab, but we're talking about a lot of jobs, a lot of folks."

Frank took a moment to finish a bite of roast beef, nodded in agreement. "That's right. Look, I'm not here to hurt your union, or your members . . . . but time marches on. Please remember I have an investment in something that certainly can be duplicated; I'd expect that there are several tech firms working on similar systems, and I can't afford endless patent fights. After all, if it is 'machine sees red light, machine tells truck to stop' that's not super science. I've got to get this going."

The three took a moment to eat, think, mull. Frank kept dipping into the pretzels, which were just the way he loved them, crunchy with minimum salt. Stewart glanced several times at his two guests but felt it best to let things develop without his intervention.

The pause continued for eating, drinking, pretzel munching, thinking. Finally Simon spoke.

"So what you want from us, from the LCTU, is to not fight this. Agree that the technology is inevitable, agree to work out totally new contracts, phase out of drivers. No battles, right?"

"No battles if something can be worked out that makes this transition as easy as possible on your members. Not up to me, up to you and the employers and no doubt Congress. I'm not a hard ass, I don't want truckers quickly out of jobs, not just like that. As I said, Social Security adjustments, early retirement, retraining . . . Simon, no doubt you've got friends in Congress. Do anything you can, we'll support, applaud. We believe the change to driverless trucks, over time, is inevitable, and not because of me or my company. I think it is a classic it will be done because it can be done."

CHAPTER TWENTY-TWO

Representative Lance Whitford rose to speak in the House. "Madam Speaker, I rise in opposition to House Bill One One Four. I've done extensive research on the proposed technology, and I can assure the members of this august body and the American public that the system, commonly known as T O T, is a safety improvement, not a hazard. T O T thinks, and reacts, faster than any human possibly can. It commands the truck to drive in the right-hand lane unless moving over for a patrol car or ambulance or driver changing a tire, never exceeding the speed limit, obeys all traffic signs and signals, and has software prepared for any contingency. It never gets sleepy, obviously never sneezes or yawns, doesn't smoke or talk on a cell phone while driving. I take nothing away from the fine, hard-working men and women who drive big rigs across this country, outstanding citizens all, but the time has come, over a period of some years, to begin easing them out from behind the wheel and letting this safe, modern, astounding technology take over transporting our goods across our highways."

Representative Josiah Williams, representative from Detroit, called Lance Whitford, representative from Maryland suburbs. "Lance, here's the situation as I see it. I've proposed one one four, keep a driver in the cab of all big rigs, even if they're just sitting there. You're pushing back against it. So there we are."

"I feel like the next line is 'may the best man win,' but I won't say it."

"I don't think either of our positions wins, not keeping drivers or dumping them fast. Compromise called for. Deal is, I've been in this game long enough to know, in the end, the most likely outcome is that the companies, the shippers and manufacturers, will set their lobbyists loose and they'll chew up the bill, your side wins. In short, I acknowledge it just ain't gonna happen, one one four will never pass. However . . . however, I can't just fold. Mainly because I want to protect jobs of drivers, many of whom live in my district, and partly because we reps don't have the option of saying 'never mind' to a position we've strongly supported. Career death."

"Agreed" said Lance.

"But I can't agree to all those jobs, hundreds of thousands of jobs, just going away as soon as the trucks can be wired up. Bad for those that lose their jobs of course, but bad for their families, mortgage payments, the whole damn economy if it happens too fast..."

"I get it, no argument. You're selling just fine, Joe. Now what?"

"Let's you and me quickly assemble a six-person special sub-committee, you pick two more, same for me, we co-chair."

When the committee assembled all knew the subject under discussion and had consulted with their staff. Also consulted, depending on the committee member's position, were the LCTU, Frank Stevenson, the FMAUF and others, so starting positions were in hand. To preemptively break any logjams before they were created, Representative Lance Whitford made an opening statement.

"Joe and I thank you for agreeing to participate. As I said to all of you, we have two positions at the far ends, and holding tight to them will be a fight, lots of emotional appeals, game playing. Joe and I are hoping you'll help us avoid that. To greatly simplify, one view is that, no matter how good or sophisticated the technology, there would always be a CDL driver in the cab, sitting there, ready to take charge. The other side started with allowing, even encouraging, the private sector to bring the technology on board as quickly as possible, drivers out of work the same, as quickly as possible. We believe neither position is viable for lots of reasons, obvious reasons. So what we are tasked with, and again our sincere thanks for your participation, is finding a proposal that will pass with as little heat, problems, as possible."

Gail South, representative from central Pennsylvania, asked "I'm not objecting to the idea, I'm here to help make it happen. But if we find what we consider to be a happy middle won't there be protests from both sides? To use your term, heat? We won't please either side, will we?"

Joe responded "No we won't, but I think we can sell it, get general acceptance, if we acknowledge both sides. Yes, jobs will be lost. Maybe we fund retraining or early retirement or targeted boosts to unemployment. Like that. And yes, we're not advocating allowing all shippers to rig up their... rigs, sorry.... as soon as possible. But obviously, way down the line, that's in everyone's best interest, best for the country to reduce shipping costs, but also best for the country to avoid the upheaval of massive layoffs of folks with good paychecks. That's our answer, but also our challenge, coming up with that middle package, one we can defend to both sides."

Gail asked "What about trucks that require the driver to do something at the delivery point? I'm thinking about auto delivery, those trailers that hold eight or nine cars, delivery usually at one dealer but maybe at more; the driver has to get the ramps ready, work with the dealership to get the cars unloaded. Or fuel deliveries. Gas stations! And trucks hauling, hell, milk or who knows what other liquid. Driver has to set the hoses, complete the delivery."

Lance responded. "No one ever said no drivers. The law won't say there can't be a driver, just that there doesn't have to be one. America will still need some drivers for some of the situations you stated. And cement trucks, and delivery of drywall and other local stuff. But sticking to long-haul, standard trailers, flatbeds, shipping containers . . . well maybe some of those deliveries won't change, like gas stations, maybe some will, with the recipients doing more."

"Such as . . . "

"Something brought by pipeline, one hose to be hooked to the liquid being hauled, maybe the industry changes so the hookups are done by employees of the receiving place, the destination. Pay less for the delivery but some of your staff have to do what a driver used to do.

Maybe the auto dealership has to do more when there is a delivery. To be discussed... lots to be discussed."

The committee met for several hours, three times. Although Josiah started by continuing his push for always a driver in the cab, he knew that wouldn't be the outcome, and so did a pro forma protest before starting to work toward the eventual outcome. In like fashion Lance started with a statement about changing to no drivers as soon as the technology and a company's money would allow, but he also backed off that fairly quickly. While he believed in his position, the recent shutdown of the bridge to Canada thoroughly convinced him that it would have to be a phasing out of drivers, or else the strikes, approved by the LCTU or not, could be nation-wide and devastating. The first proposal, the first move towards an agreement was that a trucking company could convert ten percent of its trucks to driverless a year. No driver, no observer in the cab, no human. This would allow for a gradual laying off of drivers, not a hard bump from massive layoffs in the first few years of implementation, T O T or any other similar technology that safely allowed for a driverless tractor pulling a loaded trailer. That was countered by a concern expressed by Representative Whitford: "Let's say a company has four hundred trucks. They can convert forty, then forty more, but when they drop into the three hundreds, at some point it will be only thirty, then twenty. No, that won't work, it will stretch out a program that should go faster, not slower."

The committee chewed around on that. Eventually they came up with a detailed plan that said [1] Once the amount per year was decided, it stayed at that number, so a company that could convert forty the first year could keep converting at that rate until done; [2] Companies with fewer than 100 trucks could convert at a twenty percent rate; [3] three billion dollars, with a provision for additional if needed, would be set aside for retraining or a retirement supplement for truckers losing their jobs. A key provision, one all quickly agreed to, was the creation of a grandfather clause to guarantee the paychecks of present drivers; any with at least one thousand driving hours in the last year or three thousand in the last four years would be allowed to either stay employed at the present per-mile rate, or have to be bought out based on projected earnings to age sixty-five. Companies could apply for financial relief from the government to make such buyouts happen.

What everyone on the committee realized, knew, was that a profession was disappearing, a staggering number of jobs, a seismic change in American truck delivery since the 1930s, early diesel days.

TEN YEARS LATER

Ellen Michel did move to France. She was making plans to move before the national test, so when it was over and she had received her payment Ellen was able to move after the three months it took to change her last name to Markley, during which time she lived quietly with a cousin in Alabama. Once in France she settled in, took French lessons, made friends, took up watercolor painting. After two years she met a widowed American, a retired Austin, Texas high school French instructor who had decided to live out his years in France. They married, visit America about once a year, live a good life.

James R. Dorfmann became a regular staff member of the *Sacramento True Post* not long after his reporting on the national test. He remains there today, serving as both a photographer and local-interest reporter. James and his friend Jakub have breakfast together almost every Tuesday morning of the year.

Walter "Walt" Wizniski took his earnings from the GeeCee project and joined with three of the engineers he had worked with. They established a firm that specializes in developing high-tech solutions to unusual, challenging problems in the auto, trucking, and farm equipment manufacturing industries.

Stewart Timmerlee was elected to the United States Senate from California in his second try. He is a strong advocate for truckers, working with members of the House in pushing through strong legislation to help those losing jobs due to the new technology. In doing so he works closely with Representative Josiah Williams, who continues to be elected by large margins by his pleased constituents in Detroit, and with Simon Drake, who continues to lead the LCTU.

About fifty percent of long-haul trucks are equipped with the technology. Although T O T remains the industry leader, other companies have come up with similar systems. Competition and manufacturing efficiencies have allowed the price to come down, and it is continuing to decline. At the same time the number of equipped trucks goes up steadily; close to one hundred percent in America and Canada is in the foreseeable future. Growth of use has been slower in Europe and Mexico, but it is happening.

THE END

T O T Stands for Truck Operation Technology

CAST OF CHARACTERS
IN ORDER OF APPEARANCE:

WALTER 'WALT' WIZNISKI — CHIEF PROJECT ENGINEER

ELLEN MICHEL—TEST DRIVER

FRANK STEVENSON—CEO, MHR INVESTORS, LLC

SUSAN TENNIC—PRESIDENT TENNIC PERSONNEL SERVICES

JAMES R. DORFMANN—BAKERSFIELD, CALIFORNIA PHOTOGRAPHER AND PART-TIME STRINGER FOR *THE BAKERSFIELD TRUE POST*

STEWART W. TIMMERLEE—ADMINISTRATOR OF NATIONAL HIGHWAY TRAFFIC SAFETY ADMINISTRATION—THE NHTSA

FRIEDA SHIPPENS—STEWART TIMMERLEE'S SECRETARY

JAKUB BILLSKI—JAMES'S FRIEND AT *THE BAKERSFIELD TRUE POST*

SARAH SHULMAN, NATIONAL EDITOR—*THE BAKERSFIELD TRUE POST*

SIMON DRAKE—PRESIDENT OF THE LORRY, CARRIAGE, AND TRUCKERS UNION, THE LCTU

DORIS ROSEN—SECRETARY TO SIMON DRAKE

JOSIAH (JOE) WILLIAMS—U S REPRESENTATIVE FROM DETROIT

ROBERT BANAGE—LOBBYIST FOR THE FABRICATORS, MANUFACTURERS AND ASSMBLERS UNITED FRONT, THE FMAUF

TROOPER BANKS, ARIZONA HIGHWAY PATROL

MORRIS LAYMER, FBI AGENT, WASHINGTON

PAUL AND HENRY REED—OWNERS BQD, A SMALL TRUCKING FIRM

KARL UMBLER, PAST PRESIDENT, LCTU

OREENA JONES PRESIDENT, LCTU MIDWEST DISTRICT

ROGER KROGGEN, LOBBYIST FOR CONSOLIDATED SHIPPERS AND FRIEGHTERS OF AMERICA

KYLE BRAXTON, TRUCK DRIVER, DETROIT MICHIGAN

ERIC SUDA NEW PRESIDENT, DETROIT DISTRICT, LCTU

LANCE WHITFORD—US REPRESENTATIVE FROM THE SUBURBAN LOUISVILLE, MISSOURI AREA

GAIL SOUTH—US REPRESENTATIVE FROM CENTRAL PENNSYLVANIA

A Story Of Bad:

A murder mystery and a romance wrapped around each other.

"A Story of Bad" is a highly recommended and deftly composed mystery and romance blend, for fans of either. Midwest Book Review

Winner, four out of four stars by OnLineBookClub

A Story of bad contains no graphic violence or sex

Solomon The Accountant:

A gentle love story set in a middle-class Jewish community in Toledo, Ohio in 1950.

"A surprisingly poignant novel." Cleveland Jewish News

Winner, North American Bookdealers Exchange's

Pinnacle Book Achievement Award for Fiction.

Tale Of Two Ends:

Betrayal, Divorce, Recovery.

The Author's storytelling prowess, coupled with well-developed characters makes this novel a poignant exploration of love, betrayal, and towards healing.—Honest Book Reviews Group

I bought your new book, and I am truly enjoying it and just can't seem to put it down. You write with such understanding and truth.

—An attorney and college professor

"I wish I had read this novel while I was going through my divorce."

—A reader

Edward M. Krauss is available for book clubs and other groups, no charge or fee, via Zoom. emkraussauthor@gmail.com

www.ingramcontent.com/pod-product-compliance
Lightning Source LLC
Chambersburg PA
CBHW051513260626
47162CB00008B/2947